FRANKENSTEIN

MARY SHELLEY

WORKBOOK BY SUSAN CHAPLIN

YORK PRESS

The right of Susan Chaplin to be identified as the Author of this Work has been asserted by her in accordance with the Copyright, Designs and Patents Act 1988

YORK PRESS
322 Old Brompton Road, London SW5 9JH

PEARSON EDUCATION LIMITED
Edinburgh Gate, Harlow,
Essex CM20 2JE, United Kingdom
Associated companies, branches and representatives throughout the world

First published 2016

10 9 8 7 6 5 4

ISBN 978–1–2921–3809–1

Illustrations by Rob Foote

Phototypeset by Carnegie Book Production
Printed in Slovakia

Photo credits: Popova Valeriya/Shutterstock for page 11 / Angela Rohde/ Shutterstock for page 13 / Protasov AN/Shutterstock for page 21 / Vishnevskiy Vasily/Shutterstock for page 29 / Rishiken/Shutterstock for page 33 / artsmela/ Shutterstock for page 39 / Brian A Jackson/Shutterstock for page 45 / © Alamy/ GL Archive for page 60 / © iStock/Michał Ludwiczak for page 61 / Denis Burdin/ Shutterstock for page 70

CONTENTS

PART FOUR:
THEMES, CONTEXTS AND SETTINGS

PART FIVE:
FORM, STRUCTURE AND LANGUAGE

PART SIX:
PROGRESS BOOSTER

PART ONE: GETTING STARTED

Preparing for assessment

HOW WILL I BE ASSESSED ON MY WORK ON *FRANKENSTEIN*?

All exam boards are different, but whichever course you are following, your work will be examined through these three Assessment Objectives:

Assessment Objectives	Wording	Worth thinking about ...
A01	Read, understand and respond to texts. Students should be able to: • maintain a critical style and develop an informed personal response • use textual references, including quotations, to support and illustrate interpretations.	• How well do I know what happens, what people say, do, etc? • What do I think about the key ideas in the novel? • How can I support my viewpoint in a really convincing way? • What are the best quotations to use and when should I use them?
A02	Analyse the language, form and structure used by a writer to create meanings and effects, using relevant subject terminology where appropriate.	• What specific things does the writer 'do'? What choices has Shelley made? (Why this particular word, phrase or paragraph here? Why does this event happen at this point?) • What effects do these choices create? Sympathy? Horror?
A03	Show understanding of the relationships between texts and the contexts in which they were written.	• What can I learn about society from the book? (What does it tell me about justice and prejudice, for example?) • What was society like in Shelley's time? Can I see it reflected in the text?

If you are studying OCR then you will also have a small number of marks allocated to AO4:

A04	Use a range of vocabulary and sentence structures for clarity, purpose and effect, with accurate spelling and punctuation.	• How accurately and clearly do I write? • Are there small errors of grammar, spelling and punctuation I can get rid of?

Look out for the Assessment Objective labels throughout your York Notes Workbook – these will help to focus your study and revision!

The text used in this Workbook is the Penguin Classics edition, 2003.

How to use your York Notes Workbook

There are lots of ways your Workbook can support your study and revision of *Frankenstein*. There is no 'right' way – choose the one that suits your learning style best.

1) Alongside the York Notes Study Guide and the text	2) As a 'stand-alone' revision programme	3) As a form of mock-exam
Do you have the York Notes Study Guide for *Frankenstein*? The contents of your Workbook are designed to match the sections in the Study Guide, so with the novel to hand you could: ● read the relevant section(s) of the Study Guide and any part of the novel referred to ● complete the tasks in the same section in your Workbook.	Think you know *Frankenstein* well? Why not work through the Workbook systematically, either as you finish chapters, or as you study or revise certain aspects in class or at home. You could make a revision diary and allocate particular sections of the Workbook to a day or week.	Prefer to do all your revision in one go? You could put aside a day or two and work through the Workbook, page by page. Once you have finished, check all your answers in one go! This will be quite a challenge, but it may be the approach you prefer.

HOW WILL THE WORKBOOK HELP YOU TEST AND CHECK YOUR KNOWLEDGE AND SKILLS?

Parts **Two** to **Five** offer a range of tasks and activities:

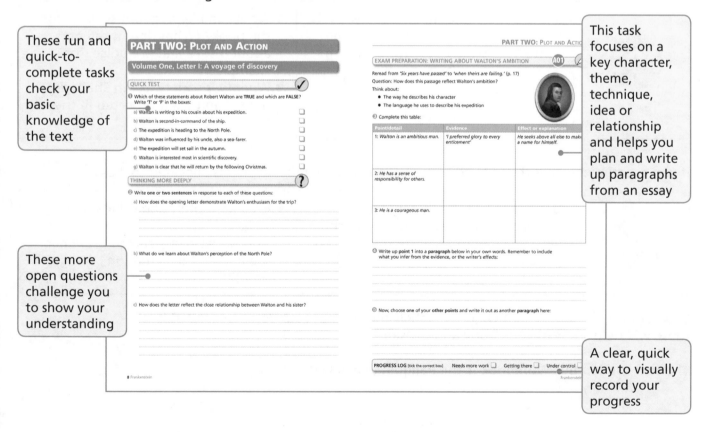

These fun and quick-to-complete tasks check your basic knowledge of the text

These more open questions challenge you to show your understanding

This task focuses on a key character, theme, technique, idea or relationship and helps you plan and write up paragraphs from an essay

A clear, quick way to visually record your progress

Each Part ends with a **Practice task** to extend your revision:

An exam-style task for you to practise a full essay

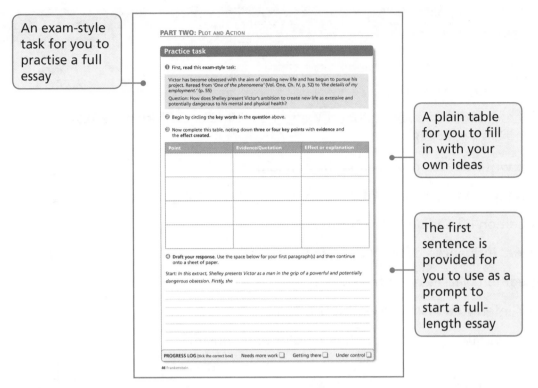

A plain table for you to fill in with your own ideas

The first sentence is provided for you to use as a prompt to start a full-length essay

Part Six: Progress Booster helps you test your own key writing skills:

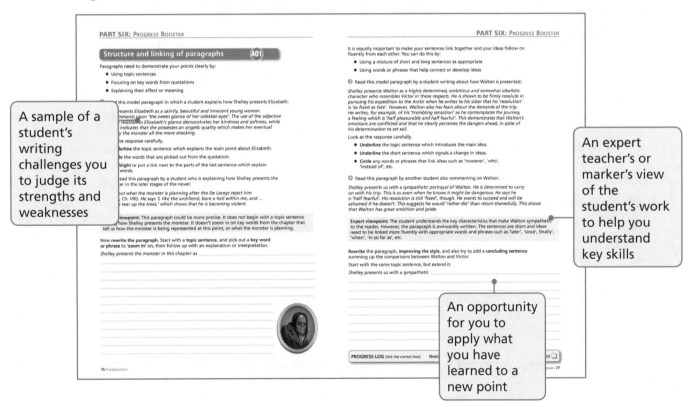

A sample of a student's writing challenges you to judge its strengths and weaknesses

An expert teacher's or marker's view of the student's work to help you understand key skills

An opportunity for you to apply what you have learned to a new point

Don't forget – these are just some examples of the Workbook contents. Inside there is much, much more to help you revise. For example:

- lots of samples of students' own work at different levels
- help with writing skills
- advice and tasks on writing about context
- a full answer key so you can check your answers
- a full-length practice exam task with guidance on what to focus on.

PART TWO: Plot and Action

Volume One, Letter I: A voyage of discovery

QUICK TEST ✓

1 Which of these statements about Robert Walton are **TRUE** and which are **FALSE**?
Write **'T'** or **'F'** in the boxes:

a) Walton is writing to his cousin about his expedition. ☐

b) Walton is second-in-command of the ship. ☐

c) The expedition is heading to the North Pole. ☐

d) Walton was influenced by his uncle, also a sea-farer. ☐

e) The expedition will set sail in the autumn. ☐

f) Walton is interested most in scientific discovery. ☐

g) Walton is clear that he will return by the following Christmas. ☐

THINKING MORE DEEPLY ?

2 Write **one** or **two sentences** in response to each of these questions:

a) How does the opening letter demonstrate Walton's enthusiasm for the trip?

b) What do we learn about Walton's perception of the North Pole?

c) How does the letter reflect the close relationship between Walton and his sister?

EXAM PREPARATION: WRITING ABOUT WALTON'S AMBITION

Reread from *'Six years have passed'* to *'when theirs are failing.'* (p. 17)

Question: How does this passage reflect Walton's ambition?

Think about:

- The way he describes his character
- The language he uses to describe his expedition

❸ Complete this table:

Point/detail	Evidence	Effect or explanation
1: *Walton is an ambitious man.*	*'I preferred glory to every enticement'*	*He seeks above all else to make a name for himself.*
2: *He has a sense of responsibility for others.*		
3: *He is a courageous man.*		

❹ Write up **point 1** into a **paragraph** below in your own words. Remember to include what you infer from the evidence, or the writer's effects:

....

....

....

....

....

❺ Now, choose **one** of your **other points** and write it out as another **paragraph** here:

....

....

....

....

....

....

PROGRESS LOG [tick the correct box]   Needs more work ☐   Getting there ☐   Under control ☐

Volume One, Letters II–III: Walton's voyage

QUICK TEST ✔

❶ **Tick** the box for the correct answer to each of these questions:

a) What quality does Walton admire in his crew?

dauntless courage ☐   navigation skills ☐   stimulating conversation ☐

b) What words does Walton use to convey his lieutenant's ambition?

'guilty of pride' ☐   'desirous of glory' ☐   'resolute and brave' ☐

c) According to Walton, which poem best captures his feelings about the trip?

The Ancient Mariner ☐   *Ode to the West Wind* ☐   *The Sea View* ☐

d) What is it that delays the trip?

technical problems ☐   illness ☐   bad weather ☐

e) What physical features of the environment suggest danger to Walton?

jagged coastline ☐   rough seas ☐   icebergs ☐

THINKING MORE DEEPLY ?

❷ Write **one** or **two sentences** in response to each of these questions:

a) Why is Walton impressed by the history of the ship's master?

....

....

....

....

....

b) Why does Walton wish he had a close friend on the ship?

....

....

....

....

....

c) What is referred to in Letter III that suggests that the trip may not end well?

....

....

....

....

....

EXAM PREPARATION: WRITING ABOUT WALTON A01

Reread from the beginning of Letter II (p. 19) to *'the happiness of her life.'* (p. 20)

Question: What does this passage reveal about Walton's state of mind?

Think about:

- Walton's situation on the ship
- Walton's sense of his own shortcomings

❸ Complete this table:

Point/detail	Evidence	Effect or explanation
1: *Walton is a sociable man and finds the ship a lonely place.*	*'I bitterly feel the want of a friend.'*	*Walton feels isolated and this depresses him, making him more welcoming of Victor later on.*
2: *Shelley sets up a comparison between Walton and the ship's lieutenant.*		
3: *Walton has a gentle, compassionate temperament.*		

❹ Write up **point 1** into a **paragraph** below in your own words. Remember to include what you infer from the evidence, or the writer's effects:

....

....

....

....

....

❺ Now, choose **one** of your other points and write it out as another **paragraph** here:

....

....

....

....

....

....

PROGRESS LOG [tick the correct box] Needs more work ☐ Getting there ☐ Under control ☐

Volume One, Letter IV: A troubled new friend

QUICK TEST ✔

❶ Which of these statements are **TRUE** and which are **FALSE**?
Write **'T'** or **'F'** in the boxes:

a) Walton's ship is halted by a blizzard. ☐

b) The crew spot a traveller moving at great speed. ☐

c) Another traveller is discovered who speaks no English. ☐

d) The traveller is a large man in robust health. ☐

e) Walton warms to the stranger immediately. ☐

f) The stranger is eager to spot the figure seen by the crew. ☐

THINKING MORE DEEPLY ?

❷ Write **one** or **two sentences** in response to each of these questions:

a) What is unusual about the physical appearance of the man spotted on the mainland before the crew find Victor?

....

....

....

....

b) How does this letter generate suspense regarding Victor's past?

....

....

....

....

c) What is important about Walton's feelings towards Victor?

....

....

....

....

....

....

EXAM PREPARATION: WRITING ABOUT THE TRAVELLERS   A01

Reread from *'About two o'clock the mist cleared'* (p. 25) to *'the fresh air, he fainted.'* (p. 26)

Question: What does this extract convey about the monster and about Victor?

Think about:

- The crew's description of the monster
- Walton's response to Victor

❸ Complete this table:

Point/detail	Evidence	Effect or explanation
1: *The monster is presented as something intriguing, almost like a wild beast or creature.*	*'This appearance excited our unqualified wonder.'*	*The figure appears almost inhuman and somewhat threatening.*
2: *Victor appears to be an educated foreigner.*		
3: *Victor is in a dangerous physical condition.*		

❹ Write up **point 1** into a **paragraph** below in your own words. Remember to include what you infer from the evidence, or the writer's effects.

....
....
....
....
....

❺ Now, choose one of your **other points** and write it out as another **paragraph** here:

....
....
....
....
....

PROGRESS LOG [tick the correct box]   Needs more work ☐   Getting there ☐   Under control ☐

Volume One, Chapter I: Frankenstein's childhood

QUICK TEST ✓

❶ Complete this **gap-fill** paragraph:

We learn that Victor's family are .... by nationality, although

Victor was born in .... His father is called ....

and his mother .... A girl named .... is

.... by Victor's parents. She is an .... from

a .... family. Victor describes his childhood as 'but one

train of .... to me'.

THINKING MORE DEEPLY ?

❷ Write **one** or **two sentences** in response to the following questions:

a) How do we learn that Victor had compassionate, loving parents?

....

....

....

....

....

b) What do we learn about Victor's feelings for Elizabeth?

....

....

....

....

....

....

c) What do we learn about Elizabeth's real father and how does he compare with Victor's father?

....

....

....

....

....

....

EXAM PREPARATION: WRITING ABOUT ELIZABETH **A01**

Reread from *'One day, when my father'* to *'among dark-leaved brambles.'* (p. 36)

Question: What is significant about the way Elizabeth's character is represented?

Think about:

- The way that Victor describes her
- How she relates to her real and foster family

❸ Complete this table:

Point/detail	Evidence	Effect or explanation
1: *Victor has a strong sense of Elizabeth's virtue.*	*She is 'heaven-sent'.*	*He describes her as an angelic creature, hinting at the strength of his feelings for her.*
2: *Victor notices that Elizabeth seems different from her foster parents.*		
3: *Elizabeth, like her real father, is portrayed as a courageous character.*		

❹ Write up **point 1** into a **paragraph** below in your own words. Remember to include what you infer from the evidence, or the writer's effects.

....

....

....

....

....

❺ Now, choose one of your **other points** and write it out as another **paragraph** here:

....

....

....

....

....

PROGRESS LOG [tick the correct box]   Needs more work ☐   Getting there ☐   Under control ☐

Volume One, Chapter II: Victor's early education

QUICK TEST ✔

❶ **Tick** the box for the correct ending to each of these sentences:

a) Henry Clerval is Victor's

closest friend ☐   cousin ☐   rival for Elizabeth's hand in marriage ☐

b) Victor has an early interest in

geology ☐   alchemy ☐   geography ☐

c) Victor grows up in

Zurich ☐   Naples ☐   Geneva ☐

d) Victor's father dismisses Victor's early reading as

'sad trash' ☐   'incomprehensible' ☐   'mere fancies' ☐

e) Victor's interest in electricity begins after

a lightning strike ☐   he reads a scientific text book ☐
a conversation with Henry ☐

THINKING MORE DEEPLY ?

❷ Write **one** or **two sentences** in response to each of these questions:

a) What comparisons can be drawn between Victor and Henry?

....
....
....
....

b) What do we learn from this chapter about Victor's passion for knowledge?

....
....
....
....

c) What does the chapter reveal about Victor's responses to nature?

....
....
....
....

EXAM PREPARATION: WRITING ABOUT VICTOR'S KEY TRAITS   **A01**

Reread from the beginning of Volume One, Chapter II to *'one among them.'* (p. 39)

Question: How are Victor's interests and traits of character represented here?

Think about:

- Victor's language in describing his thirst for knowledge
- The contrast between Victor and Elizabeth

❸ Complete this table:

Point/detail	Evidence	Effect or explanation
1: *Victor regards nature with great scientific curiosity.*	*'The world was to me a secret which I desired to divine.'*	*The word 'secret' suggests that the knowledge Victor seeks is a hidden truth, and possibly even a forbidden knowledge.*
2: *Elizabeth has a different temperament from Victor.*		
3: *Victor is something of a loner.*		

❹ Write up **point 1** into a **paragraph** below in your own words. Remember to include what you infer from the evidence, or the writer's effects:

....

....

....

....

....

❺ Now, choose one of your **other points** and write it out as another **paragraph** here:

....

....

....

....

....

....

PROGRESS LOG [tick the correct box]   Needs more work ☐   Getting there ☐   Under control ☐

Volume One, Chapters III–V: A monster is created

QUICK TEST ✓

❶ Which of these statements are **TRUE** and which are **FALSE**?
Write **'T'** or **'F'** in the boxes:

a) Victor's mother catches the fever from Elizabeth and dies. ☐

b) Victor attends university in Geneva. ☐

c) Victor is inspired by Professor Kempe. ☐

d) Victor steals bodies from the hospital for experiments. ☐

e) The monster disappears immediately after its creation. ☐

f) Victor falls ill and is nursed by Clerval. ☐

THINKING MORE DEEPLY ❓

❷ Write **one** or **two sentences** in response to each of these questions:

a) How does Chapter III reveal the closeness of Victor to his mother?

....
....
....
....
....

b) How do Chapters IV and V build up horror and suspense?

....
....
....
....
....

c) What is significant about Victor's description of the monster when it comes to life?

....
....
....
....
....

EXAM PREPARATION: WRITING ABOUT VICTOR'S DREAM A01

Reread from *'But it was in vain.'* to *'I had so miserably given life.'* (Ch. 5, p. 59)

Question: What is significant about the dream Victor has about his mother and Elizabeth?

Think about:

- How he links his mother with Elizabeth

- How he reacts to the monster when he awakes

❸ Complete this table:

Point/detail	Evidence	Effect or explanation
1: *Victor does not sleep easily after the monster's creation.*	*'I was disturbed by the wildest dreams.'*	*Victor's imagination has been profoundly unsettled by the sight of the monster.*
2: *Victor's dream connects Elizabeth with his mother.*		
3: *Victor awakes to find the monster by his bed.*		

❹ Write up **point 1** into a **paragraph** below in your own words. Remember to include what you infer from the evidence, or the writer's effects:

....

....

....

....

....

❺ Now, choose one of your **other points** and write it out as another **paragraph** here:

....

....

....

....

....

....

PROGRESS LOG [tick the correct box]   Needs more work ☐   Getting there ☐   Under control ☐

Volume One, Chapters VI–VII: News from Geneva

QUICK TEST ✔

❶ Complete this **gap-fill** paragraph:

Victor receives a letter from .... which informs him of the return

of .... to the family after some time away. Victor introduces

.... to his professors at the university in .... In

Chapter VII, Victor learns from .... about the death of

.... He makes his way back to .... During the

journey, Victor catches a glimpse of the .... The chapter ends with

Justine accused of William's ....

THINKING MORE DEEPLY ?

❷ Write **one** or **two sentences** in response to each of these questions:

a) What does Elizabeth's letter reveal about the character of Justine and her relationship to the Frankenstein family?

....

....

....

....

....

b) What is important about the way that Shelley describes the mountain landscape in Chapter VII?

....

....

....

....

....

c) What themes does Shelley introduce through the murder of William?

....

....

....

....

....

EXAM PREPARATION: WRITING ABOUT A KEY MOMENT **A01**

Reread from *'It was completely dark'* (Ch. VII, p. 77) to *'reached the summit, and disappeared.'* (p. 78)

Question: What is significant about Victor's glimpse of the monster in the mountains?

Think about:

- The nature imagery Victor uses

- His response to the sight of the monster

❸ Complete this table:

Point/detail	Evidence	Effect or explanation
1: *Victor's Romantic temperament is demonstrated by his response to the outbreak of a storm.*	*'This noble war in the sky elevated my spirits.'*	*This shows the sublime power of nature, but is also a reminder of Victor's – and mankind's – weakness in the face of natural forces.*
2: *Victor responds with horror to the glimpse of the monster.*		
3: *Victor believes the monster killed William.*		

❹ Write up **point 1** into a **paragraph** below in your own words. Remember to include what you infer from the evidence, or the writer's effects:

....

....

....

....

....

❺ Now, choose one of your **other points** and write it out as another **paragraph** here:

....

....

....

....

....

PROGRESS LOG [tick the correct box]   Needs more work ☐   Getting there ☐   Under control ☐

Volume One, Chapter VIII: Justine is executed

QUICK TEST ✔

1 **Tick** the box for the correct answer to each of these questions:

a) Victor blames himself for William's death because he

left William to go to university ☐   created the monster ☐
abandoned the monster ☐

b) A key piece of evidence against Justine is that she possesses

a miniature portrait of Caroline ☐   a miniature portrait of Alphonse ☐
a lock of William's hair ☐

c) Who gives a speech in Justine's defence?

Henry ☐   Elizabeth ☐   Victor ☐

d) Who bullies Justine into making a false confession?

a judge ☐   a fellow inmate ☐   a priest ☐

e) The public respond to Justine with

hostility ☐   sympathy ☐   indifference ☐

f) Justine is sentenced

to be deported ☐   to be hanged ☐   to be imprisoned for life ☐

THINKING MORE DEEPLY ?

2 Write **one** or **two sentences** in response to each of these questions:

a) What does this chapter reveal about the character of Elizabeth?

....

....

....

b) How does this chapter explore the justice system?

....

....

....

....

c) How does Victor respond to the trial and execution of Justine?

....

....

....

....

EXAM PREPARATION: WRITING ABOUT JUSTINE AND VICTOR **A01**

Reread from *'Justine shook her head mournfully.'* (p. 89) to *'on the scaffold as a murderess!'* (p. 90)

Question: How does this extract present Justine and Victor?

Think about:

- Justine's language
- Victor's remorse

❸ Complete this table:

Point/detail	Evidence	Effect or explanation
1: *Justine's religion is a comfort to her.*	*'God raises my weakness and gives me courage to endure the worst.'*	*Justine retains her dignity and faith, which enhances her virtue and strengthens Shelley's exploration of the justice system.*
2: *Victor is thrown into deep despair.*		
3: *Victor describes Justine in spiritual terms.*		

❹ Write up **point 1** into a **paragraph** below in your own words. Remember to include what you infer from the evidence, or the writer's effects:

....

....

....

....

....

❺ Now, choose one of your **other points** and write it out as another **paragraph** here:

....

....

....

....

....

PROGRESS LOG [tick the correct box]   Needs more work ☐   Getting there ☐   Under control ☐

Volume Two, Chapter I: Victor's remorse

QUICK TEST ✔

❶ **Tick** the box for the correct answer to each of these questions:

a) Following Justine's execution, Victor is nearly driven to:

leave his home ☐   commit suicide ☐   leave Elizabeth ☐

b) Victor refers to the monster as a:

'fiend' ☐   'devil' ☐   'ghoul' ☐

c) For how many deaths is the monster now responsible?

four ☐   one ☐   two ☐

d) To whom does Victor reveal his secret?

Henry ☐   Elizabeth ☐   nobody ☐

THINKING MORE DEEPLY ?

❷ Write **one** or **two sentences** in response to each of these questions:

a) How does the text use satanic imagery to convey Victor's despair?

....

....

....

....

....

b) Why does Victor retreat into the mountains?

....

....

....

....

....

c) What evidence is there that Victor might seek revenge against the monster?

....

....

....

....

....

....

EXAM PREPARATION: WRITING ABOUT THE LANGUAGE OF REMORSE

Reread from the beginning of Volume Two, Chapter I (p. 93) to *'the deaths of William and Justine.'* (p. 95)

Question: How does Victor express his remorse in this extract?

Think about:

- His relationship to his family
- The language Shelley uses

❸ Complete this table:

Point/detail	Evidence	Effect or explanation
1: *Victor decides against suicide for the sake of his loved ones.*	*He cannot 'leave them exposed and unprotected to the malice of the fiend'.*	*Victor feels responsible for what the monster might do next and guilty for having created this threat to his family.*
2: *Shelley uses Gothic imagery to describe Victor's despair.*		
3: *Victor feels he must avoid society.*		

❹ Write up **point 1** into a **paragraph** below in your own words. Remember to include what you infer from the evidence, or the writer's effects:

....

....

....

....

❺ Now, choose one of your **other points** and write it out as another **paragraph** here:

....

....

....

....

....

PROGRESS LOG [tick the correct box]   Needs more work ☐   Getting there ☐   Under control ☐

Volume Two, Chapter II: Victor meets his monster

QUICK TEST ✔

❶ Which of these statements are **TRUE** and which are **FALSE**?
Write **'T'** or **'F'** in the boxes:

a) Victor meets the monster in the Alps. ☐

b) The monster tries to kill Victor. ☐

c) Victor agrees to hear the monster's story. ☐

d) The two travel to a cottage in the valley. ☐

e) The monster speaks with great fluency. ☐ ☐

f) The monster feels affection and sympathy for his creator. ☐ ☐

THINKING MORE DEEPLY ❓

❷ Write **one** or **two sentences** in response to each of these questions:

a) How does this chapter create sympathy for the monster?

....
....
....
....
....
....

b) What is the significance of the landscape?

....
....
....
....
....
....

c) What evidence is there that the monster has human traits?

....
....
....
....
....
....

Reread from *'I expected this reception,'* (p. 102) to *'the work of your hands.'* (p. 104)

Question: How is the monster portrayed as sympathetic in this extract?

Think about:

- The monster's thoughts and feelings
- His connection to Victor

❸ Complete this table:

Point/detail	Evidence	Effect or explanation
1: *The monster describes his isolation.*	*'Everywhere I see bliss, from which I alone am irrevocably excluded.'*	*The monster regards himself as an outcast and is deeply distressed.*
2: *The monster begs Victor for better treatment.*		
3: *The monster condemns Victor for having created him.*		

❹ Write up **point 1** into a **paragraph** below in your own words. Remember to include what you infer from the evidence, or the writer's effects:

....

....

....

....

....

❺ Now, choose one of your **other points** and write it out as another **paragraph** here:

....

....

....

....

....

....

PROGRESS LOG [tick the correct box]   Needs more work ☐   Getting there ☐   Under control ☐

Volume Two, Chapter III: Early experiences

QUICK TEST ✓

❶ Complete this **gap-fill** paragraph:

The monster describes resting in a forest close to .... He describes

seeing the light of the .... and listening to the ....

He then travels to a village where the locals .... him. The monster

finds shelter in a .... by a cottage. He hears an old

.... playing music and is entranced by it. He observes the

family's distress and feels ....

THINKING MORE DEEPLY ?

❷ Write **one** or **two sentences** in response to each of these questions:

a) What evidence is there that the monster is overwhelmed by his early experiences?

....

....

....

....

....

....

b) What is important about the villagers' reaction to the monster?

....

....

....

....

....

....

c) What is important about the monster's reaction to the music he hears?

....

....

....

....

....

....

Reread from *'On examining my dwelling'* (p. 110) to *'unable to bear these emotions.'* (p. 111)

Question: How does Shelley use language techniques to convey the human qualities of the monster in this extract?

Think about:

- The description of sensation and emotion

- Shelley's use of first-person narration

❸ Complete this table:

Point/detail	Evidence	Effect or explanation
1: *Shelley describes the monster's pleasurable response to Old De Lacey's music.*	*'sounds sweeter than the voice of the thrush or the nightingale.'*	*Shelley uses the alliteration of 'sounds sweeter' to express the sensory pleasure the monster finds in music.*
2: *The monster's language conveys the complexity and strangeness of his new experiences.*		
3: *The monster's description of Old De Lacey shows that he believes the man to be kind, yet vulnerable.*		

❹ Write up **point 1** into a **paragraph** below in your own words. Remember to include what you infer from the evidence, or the writer's effects:

....

....

....

....

❺ Now, choose one of your **other points** and write it out as another **paragraph** here:

....

....

....

....

....

PROGRESS LOG [tick the correct box]   Needs more work ☐   Getting there ☐   Under control ☐

Volume Two, Chapter IV: The monster's education

QUICK TEST ✔

❶ **Tick** the box for the correct answer to each of these questions:

a) The family the monster observes are called:

Lacey ☐   De Beaufort ☐   De Lacey ☐

b) The father of the family is:

blind ☐   deaf ☐   unable to walk ☐

c) The monster wants to learn to:

speak ☐   dance ☐   play music ☐

d) The monster describes his reflection as:

'grotesque' ☐   'hideously distorted' ☐   'this miserable deformity' ☐

e) The old man's daughter is called:

Agnes ☐   Agatha ☐   Angela ☐

f) The monster shows kindness to the family by:

collecting firewood ☐   providing food ☐   protecting them from intruders ☐

THINKING MORE DEEPLY ?

❷ Write **one** or **two sentences** in response to each of these questions:

a) What evidence is there that kind actions come naturally to the monster?

....

....

....

....

b) What does the condition of the De Laceys' cottage reveal about them?

....

....

....

....

c) How do Agatha and Felix treat their father and what is the monster's reaction?

....

....

....

....

EXAM PREPARATION: WRITING ABOUT THE MONSTER'S CHARACTER **A01**

Reread from *'This reading had puzzled me'* (p. 116) to *'and afterwards their love.'* (p. 118)

Question: How does Shelley develop the monster's character in this extract?

Think about:

- The monster's human qualities
- The language he uses to describe himself

❸ Complete this table:

Point/detail	Evidence	Effect or explanation
1: *The monster sees his own reflection and responds with despair.*	*'I was in reality the monster that I am, I was filled with the bitterest sensations'*	*Shelley uses a pattern of three 'I's in this sentence to show how the monster sees himself as monstrous and feels excluded from the De Laceys.*
2: *The monster acts to help the family.*		
3: *The monster becomes more curious about human society.*		

❹ Write up **point 1** into a **paragraph** below in your own words. Remember to include what you infer from the evidence, or the writer's effects:

....

....

....

....

....

❺ Now, choose one of your **other points** and write it out as another **paragraph** here:

....

....

....

....

....

....

PROGRESS LOG [tick the correct box]   Needs more work ☐   Getting there ☐   Under control ☐

Volume Two, Chapters V–VI: Safie and the De Laceys

QUICK TEST ✔

❶ Which of these statements are **TRUE** and which are **FALSE**?
Write **'T'** or **'F'** in the boxes:

a) The monster sees the family welcome Safie, a young Greek girl. ☐

b) The monster discovers the De Laceys are a French family. ☐

c) Felix once helped a Turkish man escape execution. ☐

d) The Turkish man is Safie's uncle. ☐

e) The Turkish man did not keep his promise to allow Felix and Safie to marry. ☐

f) Safie escaped and found the De Lacey family. ☐

THINKING MORE DEEPLY ?

❷ Write **one** or **two sentences** in response to each of these questions:

a) What are the monster's feelings when he sees Safie welcomed by the De Lacey family?

....

....

....

....

....

b) Why was the De Lacey family banished from their country?

....

....

....

....

....

c) What evidence is there that the monster is starting to question his own family origins?

....

....

....

....

....

....

EXAM PREPARATION: WRITING ABOUT THE MONSTER'S IDENTITY   (A01)

Reread from *'These wonderful narrations'* (Ch. V, p. 122) to *'answered only with groans.'* (p. 124)

Question: How does this extract reveal the monster's growing self-awareness?

Think about:

- What the monster learns about society
- The language he uses to describe his own situation

❸ Complete this table:

Point/detail	Evidence	Effect or explanation
1: *The monster questions his identity.*	*'What was I?'*	*He becomes aware of his difference from other humans and his questions fuel his desire to learn more about his origins.*
2: *The monster learns that humans can be cruel.*		
3: *The monster wishes he had remained isolated.*		

❹ Write up **point 1** into a **paragraph** below in your own words. Remember to include what you infer from the evidence, or the writer's effects:

....
....
....
....

❺ Now, choose one of your **other points** and write it out as another **paragraph** here:

....
....
....
....
....

PROGRESS LOG [tick the correct box]   Needs more work ☐   Getting there ☐   Under control ☐

Volume Two, Chapters VII–IX: The monster's education

❶ Complete this **gap-fill** paragraph:

The monster learns to .... by collecting three books, which are

.... Lost, Lives and Sorrows of ....

By reading .... journal he learns about his own ....

He visits Old De Lacey who cannot see how the monster looks because he is

.... The old man treats the monster with ....

The rest of the family, however, are appalled by his appearance and react

by .... him away. They then leave their home, and the

monster .... down the cottage. He goes to ....

where he kills .... The monster then meets Victor and asks him

to create a .... Victor eventually .... because he

is .... by the monster's plight.

THINKING MORE DEEPLY   **?**

❷ Write **one** or **two sentences** in response to each of these questions:

a) What is the monster's reaction to reading Victor's journal?

....

....

....

....

b) Why does the monster want a female companion?

....

....

....

....

c) What evidence is there that Victor might break his promise?

....

....

....

....

EXAM PREPARATION: WRITING ABOUT VICTOR AND THE MONSTER **AO1**

Reread from *'Yet mine shall not be'* to *'change of feeling and continued.'*
(Ch. IX, p. 148)

Question: How is the relationship between the monster and Victor developed in this extract?

Think about:

- The connections between Victor and his monster

- The novel's overall themes

❸ Complete this table:

Point/detail	Evidence	Effect or explanation
1: *The monster's tale has the effect of Victor wanting to offer comfort to him, something which will have long-term implications.*	*'I was moved.'*	*Victor feels some sympathy for his creation and guilt for abandoning him.*
2: *The monster threatens violence if Victor does not meet his demands.*		
3: *The monster seeks a companion.*		

❹ Write up **point 1** into a **paragraph** below in your own words. Remember to include what you infer from the evidence, or the writer's effects:

....

....

....

....

....

❺ Now, choose one of your **other points** and write it out as another **paragraph** here:

....

....

....

....

....

....

PROGRESS LOG [tick the correct box]   Needs more work ☐   Getting there ☐   Under control ☐

Volume Three, Chapter I: Victor travels to England

QUICK TEST ✓

❶ Which of these statements are **TRUE** and which are **FALSE**?
Write 'T' or 'F' in the boxes:

a) Alphonse wishes Victor to marry Elizabeth as soon as possible. ☐

b) Victor immediately changes his mind about creating the monster's mate. ☐

c) Victor sails to England from Rotterdam. ☐

d) Victor travels to London. ☐

e) Victor travels with his university professor. ☐

f) Victor quotes a verse from a poem by Wordsworth. ☐

THINKING MORE DEEPLY ?

❷ Write **one** or **two sentences** in response to each of these questions:

a) Why is Alphonse worried about Victor?

....

....

....

....

....

b) What are Victor's feelings about creating a mate for the monster?

....

....

....

....

....

c) What impression do we get of Clerval from Victor's description of their trip?

....

....

....

....

....

EXAM PREPARATION: WRITING ABOUT HENRY CLERVAL

Reread from *'Clerval! beloved friend!'* (p. 161) to *'consoles your unhappy friend.'* (p. 162)

Question: What is significant about Victor's description of Clerval in terms of the novel's wider plot and themes?

Think about:

- The language used to describe Clerval
- Clerval's eventual fate

❸ Complete this table:

Point/detail	Evidence	Effect or explanation
1: *Like Victor, Clerval is characterised as a typical Romantic figure.*	*'His wild and enthusiastic imagination'*	*The idea of wildness suggests something uncontrolled, which links him to Victor.*
2: *Clerval's nature is kind and affectionate.*		
3: *There is a suggestion that something terrible has happened to Clerval.*		

❹ Write up **point 1** into a **paragraph** below in your own words. Remember to include what you infer from the evidence, or the writer's effects:

....
....
....
....
....

❺ Now, choose one of your **other points** and write it out as another **paragraph** here:

....
....
....
....
....
....

PROGRESS LOG [tick the correct box]   Needs more work ☐   Getting there ☐   Under control ☐

Volume Three, Chapters II–III: Victor's new creation

QUICK TEST ✓

❶ Complete this **gap-fill** paragraph:

Victor and Clerval stay in London until .... when they travel to .... They pass through .... and Oxford, and then .... and the Lake District before reaching Scotland. Victor then retires to the remote location of .... in order to create the monster's .... In Chapter III, Victor decides to .... the female creature and the .... watches him do this. The monster vows to be with Victor on his .... night. Victor sets sail and arrives in .... where he is arrested for ....

THINKING MORE DEEPLY ?

❷ Write **one** or **two sentences** in response to each of these questions:

a) What is the importance of the Lake District location in terms of the novel's wider contexts?

....

....

....

....

....

b) Why does Victor decide to destroy his second creation?

....

....

....

....

....

c) What is the monster's response to watching Victor destroy the female creation?

....

....

....

....

....

EXAM PREPARATION: WRITING ABOUT VICTOR'S CHANGE OF HEART A01

Reread from the beginning of Volume Three, Chapter III to *'the whole human race.'* (p. 171)

Question: What is significant about Victor's decision to destroy his second creation?

Think about:

- Victor's remorse and the wider theme of guilt in the novel
- The language used to describe the monster's companion

❸ Complete this table:

Point/detail	Evidence	Effect or explanation
1: *Victor begins to contemplate the consequences of his actions, and to change his mind.*	*'a train of reflection occurred to me, which led me to consider the effects'*	*Victor realises that the consequences of his actions could be disastrous.*
2: *Victor has fears that a female monster might be even more destructive than the male.*		
3: *Victor fears the two monsters might reproduce.*		

❹ Write up **point 1** into a **paragraph** below in your own words. Remember to include what you infer from the evidence, or the writer's effects:

....

....

....

....

....

❺ Now, choose one of your **other points** and write it out as another **paragraph** here:

....

....

....

....

....

....

PROGRESS LOG [tick the correct box]　　Needs more work ☐　　Getting there ☐　　Under control ☐

Volume Three, Chapter IV: Another murder trial

QUICK TEST ✓

❶ **Circle** the **themes** that are reflected in this chapter:

violence	*fatherhood*	*prejudice*
science	*ambition*	*justice system*
isolation	*love of nature*	*revenge*

❷ Now add a page reference from your copy of the book next to each circle showing where **evidence** can be found to **support** the **theme**.

THINKING MORE DEEPLY ?

❸ Write **one** or **two sentences** in response to each of these questions:

a) What are the parallels between Victor and Justine in this chapter?

....
....
....
....

b) What arouses the magistrate's suspicion that Victor is the murderer?

....
....
....
....
....
....

c) How is Alphonse represented in this chapter?

....
....
....
....
....

EXAM PREPARATION: WRITING ABOUT NARRATIVE TECHNIQUE A02

Reread from *'Mr Kirwin, on hearing this evidence'* (p. 180) to *'continually renewed the torture.'* (p. 181)

Question: How does Mary Shelley reveal Henry's fate and its consequences?

Think about:

- Victor's state of mind
- The use of a first-person narrator

❹ Complete this table:

Point/detail	Evidence	Effect or explanation
1: *Victor is initially optimistic about the outcome of the legal proceedings.*	*'I was perfectly tranquil as to the consequences of the affair.'*	*Victor's word 'tranquil' is reassuring but Shelley may hint at false optimism here, given the likely outcome.*
2: *Victor realises that the monster has killed Henry.*		
3: *Victor becomes dangerously ill after seeing the body.*		

❺ Write up **point 1** into a **paragraph** below in your own words. Remember to include what you infer from the evidence, or the writer's effects:

....
....
....
....
....

❻ Now, choose one of your **other points** and write it out as another **paragraph** here:

....
....
....
....
....

PROGRESS LOG [tick the correct box]   Needs more work ☐   Getting there ☐   Under control ☐

Volume Three, Chapters V–VI: Marriage and death

QUICK TEST ✔

❶ Which of these statements are **TRUE** and which are **FALSE**?
Write **'T'** or **'F'** in the boxes:

a) Having been found innocent, Victor travels to Paris with his father. ☐

b) Victor and Elizabeth go to Austria for their honeymoon. ☐

c) Elizabeth is killed three days after the wedding. ☐

d) Victor tries to shoot the monster. ☐

e) Alphonse dies of sorrow after hearing of the murder. ☐

f) Victor reveals the whole story to a magistrate. ☐

g) The magistrate believes that Victor is in fact the murderer. ☐

THINKING MORE DEEPLY ?

❷ Write **one** or **two sentences** in response to each of these questions:

a) How has Shelley prepared us for Elizabeth's death in Chapter VI?

....

....

....

....

b) Why does the monster kill Elizabeth rather than Victor himself?

....

....

....

....

c) How does Shelley use nature imagery to generate tension in Chapter VI?

....

....

....

....

....

EXAM PREPARATION: WRITING ABOUT THE MURDER OF ELIZABETH **A01**

Reread from *'She left me'* to *'issue from her lips.'* (Ch. VI, p. 199)

Question: How does Shelley present Elizabeth's murder?

Think about:

- The descriptions of Elizabeth in this extract
- Victor's actions and words before and after he discovers the body

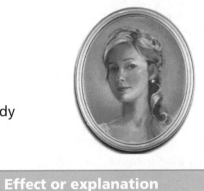

❸ Complete this table:

Point/detail	Evidence	Effect or explanation
1: Shelley presents the murder from Victor's perspective. He hears a scream and realises Elizabeth is in danger.	'As I heard it, the whole truth rushed into my mind'	Shelley conveys, through Victor's sudden understanding, that Elizabeth is the monster's target, and not Victor himself.
2: Elizabeth is presented as a blameless victim of the monster through Victor's description of her virtue.		
3: Shelley presents clear physical evidence that the monster is the murderer.		

❹ Write up **point 1** into a **paragraph** below in your own words. Remember to include what you infer from the evidence, or the writer's effects:

....

....

....

....

....

❺ Now, choose one of your **other points** and write it out as another **paragraph** here:

....

....

....

....

....

....

PROGRESS LOG [tick the correct box]   Needs more work ☐   Getting there ☐   Under control ☐

Volume Three, Chapter VII: The pursuit of the monster

QUICK TEST ✓

❶ **Tick** the box for the correct ending to each of these sentences:

a) Victor visits a graveyard to

collect body parts ☐   call on spirits to help him ☐   visit his father's grave ☐

b) Victor hears the monster

call his name ☐   scream ☐   laugh ☐

c) Victor pursues the monster to

Mont Blanc ☐   Lake Geneva ☐   the Arctic ☐

d) The chapter is narrated by Victor and then by

the Monster ☐   Walton ☐   Walton's sister ☐

e) Victor asks Walton to

destroy the monster ☐   publish Victor's story ☐   take him back to Europe ☐

f) The monster intends to

flee to another continent ☐   commit suicide ☐   live alone in the Arctic ☐

THINKING MORE DEEPLY ?

❷ Write **one** or **two sentences** in response to each of these questions:

a) How does Shelley present Victor in a sympathetic light?

....
....
....
....

b) Why is the Arctic landscape important in this chapter?

....
....
....
....

c) How does Shelley present the monster as a tragic figure?

....
....
....
....

EXAM PREPARATION: WRITING ABOUT THE LANGUAGE OF HORROR **A02**

Reread from *'Oh! when will my guiding spirit'* to *'on his persecutor.'* (p. 212)

Question: How does this extract emphasise the violent, Gothic horror of Victor's story?

Think about:

- Victor's own description of his feelings
- Walton's response to Victor's tale

❸ Complete this table:

Point/detail	Evidence	Effect or explanation
1: *Themes of vengeance and death are emphasised in the heightened language Victor uses.*	*'swear that he shall not live'*	*Victor's desire for vengeance remains and reveals his continued loathing for the monster.*
2: *Victor uses the satanic imagery of Gothic horror fiction to portray the monster as wicked.*		
3: *Walton's use of violent Gothic imagery conveys to his sister the horror of Victor's tale.*		

❹ Write up **point 1** into a **paragraph** below in your own words. Remember to include what you infer from the evidence, or the writer's effects:

....

....

....

....

....

❺ Now, choose one of your **other points** and write it out as another **paragraph** here:

....

....

....

....

....

PROGRESS LOG [tick the correct box]   Needs more work ☐   Getting there ☐   Under control ☐

Practice task

❶ First, **read** this **exam-style** task:

Victor has become obsessed with the aim of creating new life and has begun to pursue his project. Reread from *'One of the phenomena'* (Vol. One, Ch. IV, p. 52) to *'the details of my employment.'* (p. 55)

Question: How does Shelley present Victor's ambition to create new life as excessive and potentially dangerous to his mental and physical health?

❷ Begin by circling the **key words** in the **question** above.

❸ Now complete this table, noting down **three or four key points** with **evidence** and the **effect created**.

Point	Evidence/Quotation	Effect or explanation

❹ **Draft your response.** Use the space below for your first paragraph(s) and then continue onto a sheet of paper.

Start: *In this extract, Shelley presents Victor as a man in the grip of a powerful and potentially dangerous obsession. Firstly, she* ....

....

....

....

....

....

....

PROGRESS LOG [tick the correct box]   Needs more work ☐   Getting there ☐   Under control ☐

Who's who?

❶ Look at the drawings below. **Complete** the **name** of each of the characters.

Name: Robert ....

Name: Victor ....

Name: ....

Name: ....
Lavenza/Frankenstein

Name: .... Moritz

Name: Henry ....

Name: Old ....

Name: .... Frankenstein

❷ Which characters are missing from the question above? Fill in the table below:

The Frankenstein family	The De Lacey family	The tutors at Ingolstad	Others?

Robert Walton

❶ Look at these statements about Walton. For each one, decide whether it is
True [T], False [F] or whether there is **Not Enough Evidence [NEE]** to decide:

a) Walton is the novel's first narrator.   [T] [F] [NEE]

b) Walton is the navigator on a ship to the Arctic.   [T] [F] [NEE]

c) Walton has a passionate temperament.   [T] [F] [NEE]

d) Walton sympathises with Victor immediately.   [T] [F] [NEE]

e) Walton has other siblings as well as Margaret.   [T] [F] [NEE]

f) Victor tells his own story to Walton.   [T] [F] [NEE]

g) Walton never meets the monster for himself.   [T] [F] [NEE]

❷ **Complete these statements** about Walton:

a) Walton's expedition first falters because

b) Walton likes and admires Victor because

c) Walton is clearly a determined, resolute man because

d) Walton is blind to the threat of his crew's mutiny because

e) There are several parallels between Walton and Victor, such as

PROGRESS LOG [tick the correct box]   Needs more work ☐   Getting there ☐   Under control ☐

Victor Frankenstein

❶ Without looking at the book, **write down from memory** at least two pieces of information we are given about Victor in each of these areas:

a) Victor's interests as a child and young man

1: ....

....

2: ....

....

b) Victor's changing feelings towards the monster

1: ....

....

2: ....

....

c) Victor's responses to the monster's request for a companion

1: ....

....

2: ....

....

❷ Is it true that Victor is entirely **self-interested and self-absorbed**? Sort the evidence below into **'For'** and **'Against'** by **ticking** the appropriate column. You may want to tick both columns for some of the pieces of evidence.

Evidence	For	Against
He is motivated to create the monster by the prospect of glory.		
Victor insists on telling his story truthfully to Walton.		
His immediate response to the monster is one of revulsion and he abandons his creation.		
Victor agrees to create a companion for the monster.		
Victor feels responsible for the deaths of William and Justine.		
Victor feels guilt and fear after creating the monster and hides himself away.		

PROGRESS LOG [tick the correct box]   Needs more work ☐   Getting there ☐   Under control ☐

Alphonse

❶ Complete the following sentences to describe Alphonse's relationship to these characters:

a) Alphonse is Caroline's ....

b) Alphonse is Victor's ....

c) Alphonse is Elizabeth's ....

d) Alphonse is Beaufort's ....

e) Alphonse is Ernest's ....

❷ Complete this **gap-fill** paragraph about Alphonse:

Alphonse marries the daughter of his friend .... His first-born son

is called .... and he hopes to see his eldest son marry

.... who is Alphonse and Caroline's .... daughter.

Alphonse is very dismissive of Victor's interest in .... , although he

does not explain why. He is also very protective of Victor, coming to his aid when

Victor is accused of killing .... Alphonse dies shortly after the

death of ....

❸ **Write a paragraph** explaining how **Shelley presents Alphonse** as a good parent:

It is clear that Shelley wants us to see Alphonse as a good father-figure because …

....

....

....

....

....

....

....

....

....

....

....

....

....

....

....

....

| PROGRESS LOG [tick the correct box] | Needs more work ☐ | Getting there ☐ | Under control ☐ |

Elizabeth

❶ Look at this bank of **adjectives**. Circle the ones that you think best **describe** Elizabeth.

ambitious	*nurturing*	*unpredictable*	*gentle*

scheming　　　　*chaste*　　　　*jealous*

just　　　*passive*　　　*powerful*

honest　　　*insensitive*

❷ Write down **two pieces of evidence** to support each of the following points about Elizabeth:

a) Elizabeth is presented by Victor as an extremely virtuous character.

1: ....

....

2: ....

....

b) Elizabeth has a very strong sense of right and wrong.

1: ....

....

2: ....

....

c) Elizabeth is nurturing and loyal.

1: ....

....

2: ....

....

❸ Using your **own judgement**, put a mark along this line to show **Shelley's overall presentation** of Elizabeth.

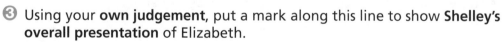

Not at all sympathetic　　　A little sympathetic　　　Quite sympathetic　　　Very sympathetic

❶　　　　　　❷　　　　　　❸　　　　　　❹

PROGRESS LOG [tick the correct box]　　Needs more work ☐　　Getting there ☐　　Under control ☐

The monster

❶ **Fill in the gaps** in these sentences about the monster:

a) The monster is .... in size.

b) The monster moves at .... speed.

c) The monster is only able to befriend Mr De Lacey because the old man
   is ....

d) The monster kills William and implicates .... in the murder.

e) The monster craves a .... companion.

f) The monster kills .... on Victor's wedding night.

g) The monster is pursued by Victor to ....

❷ **Complete these statements** about the monster, using your own judgement:

a) *In my opinion Shelley presents the monster sympathetically, for example when* ....

....

....

....

....

b) *In my opinion, the monster is not entirely to blame for the murders he
   commits because* ....

....

....

....

....

c) *I believe that Victor has mixed feelings about the monster because* ....

....

....

....

....

....

❸ Using your **own judgement**, put a mark along this line to show **Shelley's overall
presentation** of the monster.

Not at all sympathetic	A little sympathetic	Quite sympathetic	Very sympathetic
❶	❷	❸	❹

PROGRESS LOG [tick the correct box]   Needs more work ☐   Getting there ☐   Under control ☐

Henry Clerval, William Frankenstein, Old De Lacey

❶ Which character? **Tick** the character that each quotation refers to:

Quotation	Henry	William	Old De Lacey
'of singular talent and fancy'			
'laughing blue eyes, dark eyelashes, and curling hair'			
'descended from a good family in France'			

❷ Write **one** or **two sentences** in response to each of these questions:

a) How do we know that, like Victor, Henry is a passionate, Romantic character?

....

....

....

b) Why is the death of William a turning point in the novel?

....

....

....

c) How does Old De Lacey compare to other father-figures in the novel?

....

....

....

❸ Which of these three characters:

a) Briefly befriends the monster? ....

b) Studies at Ingolstad? ....

c) Is murdered because he refuses to befriend the monster? ....

| PROGRESS LOG [tick the correct box] | Needs more work ☐ | Getting there ☐ | Under control ☐ |

Caroline Beaufort, Justine Moritz, Safie

❶ Complete the following **sentences**:

a) Caroline's father was the best friend of .... Frankenstein.

b) Caroline becomes the adoptive mother of ....

c) Justine is a servant in the .... household.

d) Justine is falsely convicted of the murder of ....

e) Safie is the daughter of a .... merchant.

f) Safie falls in love with ....

❷ Tick the appropriate columns to show which term applies to which character. Some terms will apply to all three.

Term	Caroline	Justine	Safie
a servant			
loyal			
compassionate			
honest			
married			
a mother			
courageous			
proud			
gentle			
ambitious			
wealthy			

PROGRESS LOG [tick the correct box]   Needs more work ☐   Getting there ☐   Under control ☐

Practice task

❶ First, **read** this **exam-style** task:

Reread from the beginning of Volume Two, Chapter VII (p. 130) to *'that inconstant shade.'* (p. 133)

Question: How does Shelley present the monster as a sympathetic, human creature in this extract, and in the novel as a whole?

❷ Begin by circling the **key words** in the **question** above.

❸ Now complete this table, noting down **three or four key points** with **evidence** and the **effect created**.

Point	Evidence/Quotation	Effect or explanation

❹ **Draft your response.** Use the space below for your first paragraph(s) and then continue onto a sheet of paper.

Start: *In this extract, Shelley presents the monster as a sympathetic creature possessing many human qualities. Firstly, she* ....

....

....

....

....

....

....

....

....

PROGRESS LOG [tick the correct box]   Needs more work ☐   Getting there ☐   Under control ☐

Themes

❶ **Circle** the **themes** you think are most relevant to *Frankenstein*:

revenge	*love*	*social class*
ambition	*knowledge*	*childhood*
isolation	*power*　*war*	*nature*
Romanticism	*justice*	*poverty*
companionship	*travel*	*prejudice*

❷ Consider the **relationships** between the following **characters** and write down which **theme or themes** they reflect:

a) Victor and the monster ....

b) Victor and Clerval ....

c) The monster and William ....

d) Safie's father and Felix ....

e) Justine and Elizabeth ....

f) Walton and his crew ....

g) The monster and the villagers ....

THINKING MORE DEEPLY ❓

❸ Thinking about the **themes** of **revenge** and **ambition**, write **one** or **two sentences** in response to each of these questions:

a) What sort of parallels does Shelley draw between Walton and Victor?

....

....

....

....

....

b) What sort of comparisons are there between Victor and his monster?

....

....

....

....

....

❹ Give three examples from the novel that illustrate the **theme** of **isolation**.

a) ....

....

b) ....

....

c) ....

....

❺ Consider the following examples from the text and, using your own judgement, describe which theme or themes they relate to and why:

a) Walton's journey to the north pole relates to the theme of ....

because ....

....

....

....

b) Victor's decision to create a female companion for the monster relates to the theme of ....

because ....

....

....

....

c) The monster's murder of Clerval relates to the theme of ....

because ....

....

....

....

d) Elizabeth's role in the trial of Justine relates to the theme of ....

because ....

....

....

....

⑥ Complete the following **sentences** about the **theme of prejudice**:

a) Justine is tormented by the crowd before her execution because ....

....

....

b) Victor abandons his creation because ....

....

....

c) The De Laceys run away from the monster because ....

....

....

d) Safie's father is condemned to death because ....

....

....

❼ Think about the following themes:

isolation   **revenge**   **knowledge**   **sense of justice**

a) Using your **own judgement**, rate each character from 1 (low) to 5 (high) in terms of their importance to each of these themes:

	Isolation	Revenge	Knowledge	Sense of justice
Victor				
Walton				
The monster				
Felix De Lacey				

b) Now write **one** or **two sentences** saying which **two characters** from the list in the table best illustrate the **theme of isolation** and why:

....

....

....

....

....

Reread from *'Oh, Frankenstein'* to *'Listen to me, Frankenstein.'* (Vol. Two, Ch. II, p. 103)

Question: How does the monster's conversation with Victor illustrate the theme of justice?

Think about:

- The monster's accusations
- The monster's description of his suffering

⑧ Complete this table:

Point/detail	Evidence	Effect or explanation
1: *The monster's suffering highlights Victor's injustice.*	*'be not equitable to every other, and trample upon me alone, to whom thy justice, and even thy clemency and affection, is most due.'*	*The monster appeals directly to Victor's sense of justice as the creator of a being that deserves the compassion due from a father to a child.*
2: *The monster believes Victor should make amends.*		
3: *The monster seeks Victor's love.*		

⑨ Write up **point 1** into a **paragraph** below in your own words. Remember to include what you infer from the evidence, or the writer's effects:

....

....

....

....

....

⑩ Now, choose one of your **other points** and write it out as another **paragraph** here:

....

....

....

....

....

....

PROGRESS LOG [tick the correct box]   Needs more work ☐   Getting there ☐   Under control ☐

Contexts

QUICK TEST ✔

❶ **Tick** the box for the correct answer to each of these questions:

a) Who was the famous philosopher father of Mary Shelley?

William Wordsworth ☐   Thomas Godwin ☐   William Godwin ☐

b) What was the first name of the Romantic poet to whom Mary Shelley was married?

John ☐   Percy ☐   Samuel ☐

c) Who in 1802 conducted experiments on animal parts using electrical currents?

Galvani ☐   Aldini ☐   Priestley ☐

d) To which mythical figure is Victor compared?

Achilles ☐   Icarus ☐   Prometheus ☐

e) Which poem is quoted as the epigraph to Shelley's novel?

Paradise Lost ☐   *Paradise Regained* ☐   *The Prelude* ☐

f) Which literary movement of the early nineteenth century provided inspiration for Shelley's novel?

Neo-Classicism ☐   Realism ☐   Romanticism ☐

g) Which play provides a template for Shelley's novel?

Macbeth ☐   *Faust* ☐   *The Changeling* ☐

h) Where was Mary Shelley when she began to write *Frankenstein*?

Geneva ☐   Ingolstad ☐   London ☐

THINKING MORE DEEPLY ?

❷ Write **one** or **two sentences** in response to each of these questions:

a) How did the scientific discoveries of Shelley's period influence her novel?

....

....

....

....

....

....

....

....

....

b) Why does Shelley describe Victor as a 'Modern Prometheus'?

....

....

....

....

....

....

c) How does Shelley's novel allude to the religious theme of the 'Fall of Man'?

....

....

....

....

....

....

....

❸ The Gothic novel was popular during Shelley's time and **Gothic imagery** features frequently in the text. **Provide a quotation** from the text showing how Gothic imagery is used in relation to the following:

a) The creation of the monster

....

....

....

....

....

b) The monster's desire for revenge

....

....

....

....

....

c) The landscape in which Victor and the monster first meet

....

....

....

....

....

PROGRESS LOG [tick the correct box]   Needs more work ☐   Getting there ☐   Under control ☐

Settings

QUICK TEST

❶ Look at the illustrations below. **Complete the names** of the key locations that appear in *Frankenstein*:

The A...................................

E ....

B ....,

G ....

I ....

P ....

I ....

The O ....

I ....

The A...................................

D..

L..

C..

❷ **Name one event** that occurs in each of the following settings:

a) The Alps ....

b) Ingolstad ....

c) Ireland ....

THINKING MORE DEEPLY   **?**

❸ Write **one** or **two sentences** in response to each of these questions:

a) How does Shelley's description of the Alps reflect the sublime power of nature?

....

....

....

....

b) How is the theme of knowledge expressed through Walton's journey to the Arctic?

....

....

....

....

c) Which of the novel's themes are highlighted by the setting of the Irish prison?

....

....

....

....

❹ Choose a further setting from the novel and write a paragraph outlining how Shelley describes it and its significance to the novel as a whole.

....

....

....

....

....

....

....

....

....

....

....

....

....

PROGRESS LOG [tick the correct box]   Needs more work ☐   Getting there ☐   Under control ☐

Practice task

❶ First, **read** this **exam-style** task:

Reread from *'I expected this reception'* (Vol. Two, Ch. II, p. 102) to the end of the chapter.

Question: Starting with this extract, explore the theme of justice. Refer closely to the extract in your answer and then write about how the theme is presented in the rest of the novel.

❷ Begin by circling the **key words** in the **question** above.

❸ Now complete this table, noting down **three or four key points** with **evidence** and the **effect created**.

Point	Evidence/Quotation	Effect or explanation

❹ **Draft your response.** Use the space below for your first paragraph(s) and then continue onto a sheet of paper.

Start: *In this extract, Shelley presents the monster as pleading for justice with his creator. Firstly, she* ....

....

....

....

....

....

....

....

....

PROGRESS LOG [tick the correct box]   Needs more work ☐   Getting there ☐   Under control ☐

PART FIVE: FORM, STRUCTURE AND LANGUAGE

Form

❶ **Tick** the box for the correct answer to each of these questions:

   a) How many volumes is the novel divided into?

   two ☐   five ☐   three ☐

   b) The narrator who begins and ends the novel is:

   Walton ☐   Victor ☐   Walton's sister ☐

   c) The monster's experiences in Volume Two are narrated by:

   the monster to Victor ☐   the monster to Walton ☐   Walton to his sister ☐

   d) Victor's experience in prison is narrated by:

   Victor to Walton ☐   Victor to Elizabeth ☐   Walton to his sister ☐

❷ Complete the following sentences so that they reveal the Chinese box-style narration of the novel:

   a) Walton's story is told to ....

   b) Victor's story is told to ....

   c) The monster's story is told to .... who tells it
     to ....

   d) The reader learns of Justine's story through ....
     and then ....

   e) The reader learns of the monster's presence in the Arctic
     through ....

❸ Write **one or two sentences** in response to this question:

   a) How does the form of the novel help to create a sense of realism for the reader?

....

....

....

....

....

....

....

....

PROGRESS LOG [tick the correct box]   Needs more work ☐   Getting there ☐   Under control ☐

Structure

1 Which of these statements about the structure of the text are **TRUE** and which are **FALSE**? Write 'T' or 'F' in the boxes:

a) The monster is created in Volume Two of the novel. ☐

b) Justine does not appear in the text after Volume One. ☐

c) Volume One ends with Victor meeting the monster in the Alps. ☐

d) Volume Two ends with Victor agreeing to create another monster. ☐

e) Volume Three begins with Victor travelling to London. ☐

f) Clerval does not appear in the text in Volume Three. ☐

g) Two deaths are narrated in Volume Three, Chapter VI. ☐

2 **Number** these events so that they are in the **correct chronological sequence**. Use 1 for the first event and 8 for the final event.

a) Victor goes to university. ☐

b) Victor's mother dies. ☐

c) Justine is executed. ☐

d) Victor creates the monster. ☐

e) Victor travels to London with Clerval. ☐

f) William is murdered. ☐

g) Victor marries Elizabeth. ☐

h) Walton meets the monster. ☐

3 Write a **paragraph** explaining why it is important that Walton's first-person narrative to his sister introduces and closes the novel:

....

....

....

....

....

....

....

....

....

EXAM PREPARATION: WRITING ABOUT STRUCTURE

Reread from *'The different accidents of life'* (Vol. One, Ch. V, p. 58) to *'Dante could not have conceived.'* (p. 58)

Question: How does this extract relate back to key events that have happened, and foreshadow events to come?

Think about:

- How Victor dreams of Elizabeth
- How he describes the monster when he awakes

❸ Complete this table:

Point	Evidence/Quotation	Effect or explanation
1: *Victor's dream of Elizabeth foreshadows his wedding night.*	*'I embraced her, but as I imprinted the first kiss on her lips, they became livid with the hue of death'*	*This anticipates Elizabeth's death on her wedding night.*
2: *Elizabeth is linked to Victor's mother.*		
3: *From the moment of its creation, Victor perceives the monster as a great threat to him.*		

❹ Write up **point 1** into a **paragraph** below in your own words. Remember to include what you infer from the evidence, or the writer's effects:

....

....

....

....

❺ Now, choose one of your **other points** and write it out as another **paragraph** here:

....

....

....

....

....

PROGRESS LOG [tick the correct box]   Needs more work ☐   Getting there ☐   Under control ☐

Language

QUICK TEST

❶ Out of the following images, circle those which are examples of **Gothic imagery**:

'evil spirit' (Vol. One, Ch. I, p. 93)	'sad trash' (Vol. One, Ch. II, p. 40)
'uncouth man' (Vol. One, Ch. III, p. 47)	'shrivelled complexion' (Vol. One, Ch. V, p. 58)
'celestial spirit' (Vol. One, Letter IV, p. 30)	'archfiend' (Vol. Two, Ch. VIII, p. 138)

'mountains of ice' (Vol. Three, Ch. VII, p. 215)

'miserable deformity' (Vol. Two, Ch. IV, p. 117)   'grave-worms crawling' (Vol. One, Ch. V, p. 59)

THINKING MORE DEEPLY

❷ Write a **sentence** explaining the effects of Shelley's use of **adverbs** or **adjectives** in these quotations:

a) 'I trembled excessively' (Vol. One, Ch. V, p. 61)

....

....

....

b) 'Was man, indeed, at once so powerful, so virtuous, and magnificent, yet so vicious and base?' (Vol. Two, Ch. V, p. 122)

....

....

....

❸ Write a **sentence** explaining the effect of these **metaphors** to describe Victor:

a) A 'gallant vessel' that is 'wrecked' (Vol. One, Letter IV, p. 32)

....

....

....

b) Victor's passion for knowledge is a 'torrent which, in its course, has swept away all my hopes and joys' (Vol. One, Ch. II, p. 40).

....

....

....

❹ Using your **own judgement**, **complete** the following short **paragraphs** about Shelley's use of language:

a) *In my opinion, Shelley's use of sublime nature imagery is important because ...*

....

....

....

....

....

....

....

....

....

....

b) *I believe that the reason Shelley makes the monster speak so eloquently is ...*

....

....

....

....

....

....

....

....

....

....

c) *In my opinion, Victor's use of Gothic imagery to describe his creation has the effect of ...*

....

....

....

....

....

....

....

....

....

....

EXAM PREPARATION: WRITING ABOUT LANGUAGE

Question: *Discuss how Shelley uses various images to convey the theme of isolation in the novel.*

Think about:

- Walton's journey to the Arctic
- Representations of Victor and the monster

⑤ Complete this table:

Point	Evidence/Quotation	Effect or explanation
1: *The language emphasises how isolated Walton will be in a bleak and inhospitable landscape.*	*'I am going to unexplored regions to "the land of mist and snow"'*	*This symbolises Walton's retreat from civilisation, something which Victor also pursues.*
2: *Nature imagery features heavily in the description of Victor's meeting with the monster.*		
3: *The monster uses Gothic imagery to describe himself.*		

⑥ Write up **point 1** into a **paragraph** below in your own words. Remember to include what you infer from the evidence, or the writer's effects:

....

....

....

....

....

⑦ Now, choose **one** of your **other points** and write it out as another **paragraph** here:

....

....

....

....

....

PROGRESS LOG [tick the correct box]   Needs more work ☐   Getting there ☐   Under control ☐

Practice task

❶ First, **read** this **exam-style** task:

Reread from the beginning of Volume One, Chapter V, p. 58 to *'Dante could not have conceived.'* (p. 59)

Question: How does Shelley use the language, imagery and symbolism associated with Gothic writing in this extract and at other times in the novel?

❷ Begin by circling the **key words** in the **question** above.

❸ Now complete this table, noting down **three or four key points** with **evidence** and the **effect created**.

Point	Evidence/Quotation	Effect or explanation

❹ **Draft your response.** Use the space below for your first paragraph(s) and then continue onto a sheet of paper.

Start: *In this extract, Shelley uses a great deal of the language, imagery and symbolism of the Gothic. Firstly, she* ....

....

....

....

....

....

....

....

PROGRESS LOG [tick the correct box]　　Needs more work ☐　　Getting there ☐　　Under control ☐

PART SIX: PROGRESS BOOSTER

Expressing and explaining ideas (A01) (A04)*

❶ How well can you express your ideas about *Frankenstein*? Look at this grid and tick the level you think you are currently at:

Level	How you respond	Writing skills	Tick
High	• You analyse the effect of specific words and phrases very closely (i.e. 'zooming in' on them and exploring their meaning). • You select quotations very carefully and you embed them fluently in your sentences. • You are persuasive and convincing in the points you make, often coming up with original ideas.	• You use a wide range of specialist terms (words like 'imagery'), excellent punctuation, accurate spelling, grammar, etc.	
Mid/ Good	• You analyse some parts of the text closely, but not all the time. • You support what you say with evidence and quotations, but sometimes your writing could be more fluent to read. • You make relevant comments on the text.	• You use a good range of specialist terms, generally accurate punctuation, usually accurate spelling, grammar, etc.	
Lower	• You comment on some words and phrases but often you do not develop your ideas. • You sometimes use quotations to back up what you say but they are not always well chosen. • You mention the effect of certain words and phrases but these are not always relevant to the task.	• You do not have a very wide range of specialist terms, but you have reasonably accurate spelling, punctuation and grammar.	

SELECTING AND USING QUOTATIONS

❷ Read these two samples from students' responses to a question about how **Victor** is presented. Decide which of the three levels they fit best, i.e. **lower** (L), **mid** (M) or **high** (H).

Student A: *Victor is named by Shelley as a 'Modern Prometheus' which alerts the reader to his capacity for over-reaching ambition. Prometheus is the Greek mythical hero who stole fire from the gods, and who was punished accordingly. In creating the monster, Victor in a sense steals from God the power of generating life; he states that he wishes to uncover 'the secrets of heaven and earth', and to master the 'hidden laws' of nature. The use of the terms 'secret' and 'hidden' suggest that what Victor seeks is a knowledge beyond the proper bounds of human understanding and, like Prometheus, he suffers for his excessive ambition.*

Level ? ☐ Why? ....

....

Student B: *Victor is too ambitious in trying to create life, and this is why he is compared to the Greek hero Prometheus who was punished for stealing fire from the gods. Victor is punished for creating life and 'playing God', because his monster turns against him and kills the people he loves. Victor fails to see that nature's 'secrets' should remain hidden, until it is too late.*

Level ? ☐ Why? ....

....

*AO4 is assessed by OCR only.

ZOOMING IN – YOUR TURN!

Here is the first part of another student response. The student has picked a good quotation, but she/he hasn't 'zoomed in' on any particular words or phrases:

After Victor creates the monster, he becomes very disturbed by its appearance. He states that, 'the beauty of the dream vanished, and breathless horror and disgust filled my heart'. He is determined to reject his hideous creation.

❸ Pick out one of the **words** or **phrases** the student has quoted and write a further sentence to complete the explanation:

The word/phrase '.................................' suggests that ....

....

EXPLAINING IDEAS

You need to be very precise about the way Shelley expresses ideas, which can be done by varying your use of verbs (not just using 'says' or 'means').

❹ Read this paragraph from a **mid-level** student response to a question about Victor's relationship with the monster. Circle all the **verbs** that are repeated (not in the quotations):

The author uses landscape in this chapter to show how the monster and Victor are isolated from the rest of humanity. The text says that the scene is 'terrifically desolate' and the mountains 'admit of no escape'. This shows how Victor and the monster are thrown together almost within a natural prison. Shelley says here how the two of them are locked together in a desolate struggle, and shows how excluded they are from civilisation.

❺ Now choose some of the words below to replace your circled ones:

implies	*demonstrates*	*reveals*	*states*
conveys	*indicates*	*suggests*	

❻ Rewrite your **high-level** version of the paragraph in full below. Remember to mention the **author by name** to show you understand she is **making choices** in how she presents characters, themes and events.

....

....

....

....

....

....

PROGRESS LOG [tick the correct box]   Needs more work ☐   Getting there ☐   Under control ☐

Making inferences and interpretations

WRITING ABOUT INFERENCES

You need to be able to show you can read between the lines, and make inferences rather than just explain more explicit 'surface' meanings.

Here is an extract from one student's **high-level** response to a question about the monster's education and how this is presented:

The monster's encounter with the De Lacey family allows him to appreciate the benevolence of human nature, whilst the family's misfortune shows him that men can be vicious too. The monster also learns that the conflict between virtue and vice which exists within humanity also exists within himself, since he becomes envious of the De Laceys. The text implies that this is why the monster can identify with Satan when he reads 'Paradise Lost'; like Satan, who is jealous of Adam in paradise, the monster feels 'the bitter gall of envy' as he reflects on the 'bliss' of the family compared with his own isolation.

❶ Look at the response carefully.

- **Underline** the simple point which explains how the De Laceys contribute to the monster's education.

- **Circle** the sentence that develops the first point.

- **Highlight** the sentence that shows an inference and begins to explore wider interpretations.

INTERPRETING – YOUR TURN!

❷ Read the opening to this student response carefully and then **choose the sentence** from the list which shows **inference** and could lead to a **deeper interpretation**. Remember – interpreting is *not* guesswork!

When the monster meets William, his intention is not to murder him. Instead, the monster hopes that William will offer friendship and acceptance because he has 'lived too short a time to have imbibed a horror of deformity'. This suggests that children have an innocent and open-minded approach to others. It also implies that …

    a) *the monster thinks of himself as deformed.*

    b) *people become less accepting of difference as they age.*

    c) *the monster feels hopeful about becoming friends with William.*

❸ Now complete this **paragraph** about Walton, adding your own final sentence which makes inferences or explores interpretations:

Walton wishes to make a name for himself by travelling to the Arctic to make scientific discoveries. He wants in particular to uncover 'the secret of the magnet'. This implies that Walton is in some ways comparable to Victor because ....

....

....

....

PROGRESS LOG [tick the correct box]   Needs more work ☐   Getting there ☐   Under control ☐

Writing about context

EXPLAINING CONTEXT

When you write about context, you must make sure it is relevant to the task.

Read this comment by a student about Victor:

Victor's fascination with science, coupled with his intensely passionate nature, contribute to his obsessive interest in the origin and creation of life. Victor's scientific pursuits very much reflect the concerns of Shelley's time in that scientists, such as Luigi Galvani, were conducting experiments with electricity. Victor's emotional, rather volatile temperament also makes it difficult for him to moderate his passions, and this links Victor and the text as a whole to the movement known as Romanticism.

❶ Why is this an effective paragraph about context? Select a), b) or c).

a) Because it explains that Victor is obsessive about science.

b) Because it shows how Victor's interests and characteristics relate to the culture of Shelley's period.

c) Because it tells us a key fact about the scientist Luigi Galvani.

EXPLAINING – YOUR TURN!

❷ Now read this further paragraph and complete it by choosing a suitable point related to context from a), b) or c) below:

The monster refers to the De Laceys' residence as a 'paradise' and is drawn towards the family's 'gentle manners and beauty'. They seem to be untouched by the vices that the monster starts to learn are very much a part of wider human society. This theme of innocence, and the contrast between vice and virtue reflects …

a) *how the characters in the novel are either very good, or very bad.*

b) *how much the monster is starting to learn about human society.*

c) *the Romantic philosopher Rousseau's influential belief that human beings are born virtuous, but eventually become corrupted by society.*

❸ Now, write a paragraph explaining how Shelley shows the importance of education and environment in the formation of character:

Shelley demonstrates the importance of a good education ....

....

....

....

....

....

....

PROGRESS LOG [tick the correct box]   Needs more work ☐   Getting there ☐   Under control ☐

Structure and linking of paragraphs (A01)

Paragraphs need to demonstrate your points clearly by:

- Using topic sentences
- Focusing on key words from quotations
- Explaining their effect or meaning

❶ Read this model paragraph in which a student explains how Shelley presents Elizabeth:

Shelley presents Elizabeth as a saintly, beautiful and innocent young woman. Victor comments upon 'the sweet glance of her celestial eyes'. The use of the adjective 'sweet' in relation to Elizabeth's glance demonstrates her kindness and softness, while 'celestial' indicates that she possesses an angelic quality which makes her eventual murder by the monster all the more shocking.

Look at the response carefully.

- **Underline** the topic sentence which explains the main point about Elizabeth.
- **Circle** the words that are picked out from the quotation.
- **Highlight** or put a tick next to the parts of the last sentence which explain the words.

❷ Now read this paragraph by a student who is explaining how Shelley presents the monster in the later stages of the novel:

We find out what the monster is planning after the De Laceys reject him (Vol. Two, Ch. VIII). He says 'I, like the archfiend, bore a hell within me, and … wished to tear up the trees,' which shows that he is becoming violent.

Expert viewpoint: This paragraph could be more precise. It does not begin with a topic sentence stating how Shelley presents the monster. It doesn't zoom in on key words from the chapter that tell us how the monster is being represented at this point, or what the monster is planning.

Now **rewrite the paragraph**. Start with a **topic sentence**, and pick out a **key word or phrase** to **'zoom in'** on, then follow up with an explanation or interpretation.

Shelley presents the monster in this chapter as ....

....

....

....

....

....

....

....

....

....

....

....

It is equally important to make your sentences link together and your ideas follow on fluently from each other. You can do this by:

- Using a mixture of short and long sentences as appropriate
- Using words or phrases that help connect or develop ideas

❸ Read this model paragraph by a student writing about how Walton is presented:

Shelley presents Walton as a highly determined, ambitious and somewhat idealistic character who resembles Victor in these respects. He is shown to be firmly resolute in pursuing his expedition to the Arctic when he writes to his sister that his 'resolution' is 'as fixed as fate'. However, Walton also has fears about the demands of the trip. He writes, for example, of his 'trembling sensation' as he contemplates the journey, a feeling which is 'half pleasurable and half fearful'. This demonstrates that Walton's emotions are conflicted and that he clearly perceives the dangers ahead, in spite of his determination to set sail.

Look at the response carefully.

- **Underline** the topic sentence which introduces the main idea.
- **Underline** the short sentence which signals a change in ideas.
- **Circle** any words or phrases that link ideas such as 'however', 'who', 'instead of', etc.

❹ Read this paragraph by another student also commenting on Walton:

Shelley presents us with a sympathetic portrayal of Walton. He is determined to carry on with his trip. This is so even when he knows it might be dangerous. He says he is 'half fearful'. His resolution is still 'fixed', though. He wants to succeed and will be ashamed if he doesn't. This suggests he would 'rather die' than return shamefully. This shows that Walton has great ambition and pride.

Expert viewpoint: The student understands the key characteristics that make Walton sympathetic to the reader. However, the paragraph is awkwardly written. The sentences are short and ideas need to be linked more fluently with appropriate words and phrases such as 'later', 'since', finally', 'when', 'in so far as', etc.

Rewrite the paragraph, **improving the style**, and also try to add a **concluding sentence** summing up the comparisons between Walton and Victor.

Start with the same topic sentence, but extend it:

Shelley presents us with a sympathetic ....

....

....

....

....

....

....

....

....

PROGRESS LOG [tick the correct box]   Needs more work ☐   Getting there ☐   Under control ☐

Writing skills (A01) (A04)*

Here are a number of key words you might use when writing in the exam:

Content and structure	Characters and style	Linguistic features
volume	character	metaphor
chapter	sympathetic	imagery
quotation	heroic	personification
extract	flawed	symbol
episode	minor (character)	juxtaposition
development	tragedy	parallel
dialogue	Romantic	comparison
narration	ambitious	foreshadowing

❶ Circle any you might find difficult to spell, and then use the 'Look, Say, Cover, Write, Check' method to learn them. This means: **look** at the word; **say** it out loud; then **cover** it up; **write** it out; uncover and **check** your spelling with the correct version.

❷ Create a **mnemonic** for five of your difficult spellings. For example:

tragedy: **t**en **r**eally **a**ngry **g**irls **e**njoyed **d**ancing **y**esterday! Or …

break the word down: T – RAGE – DY!

a) ....

b) ....

c) ....

d) ....

e) ....

❸ Circle any **incorrect spellings** in this paragraph and then rewrite it:

At the end of Volume One, Justine is put on trial for the murder of Wiliam. She is not able to explain how she came to have the portrate of Caroline and this is strong evidense against her. She is also forced into making a false confesion and is eventually excecuted for the crime. The reader knows that Justine is inocent and that the monster in fact killed Wiliam.

....

....

....

....

....

*AO4 is assessed by OCR only.

④ **Punctuation** can help make your meaning clear.

Here is one response by a student commenting on Shelley's use of sublime imagery to describe landscape. Check for correct use of:

- Apostrophes
- Speech marks for quotations and emphasis
- Full stops, commas and capital letters

Shelleys use of sublime imagery allows her to represent the power and desolation of the natural landscape by placing victor in this landscape shelley makes the reader more aware of his isolation. The landscape is described as terrifically desolate and its magnitude and grandeur are emphasised through the use of words such as immense and magnificent.

Rewrite it **correctly** here:

....

....

....

....

....

⑤ It is better to use the **present tense** to describe what is happening in the novel.

Look at these two extracts. Which one uses tenses **consistently** and **accurately**?

Student A: *One of the techniques that Shelley used to represent Victor was to draw a series of contrasts and comparisons between Victor and other key characters. For instance, Shelley depicted Clerval as a Romantic, passionate man and this is similar to Victor. Clerval, though, was more moderate in his passions and therefore less likely to be driven to destructive extremes.*

Student B: *One of the techniques that Shelley uses to represent Victor is to draw a series of contrasts and comparisons between Victor and other key characters. For instance, Shelley depicts Clerval as a Romantic, passionate man and this is similar to Victor. Clerval, though, is more moderate in his passions and therefore less likely to be driven to destructive extremes.*

⑥ Now look at this further paragraph. **Underline** or **circle** all the **verbs** first.

Shelley represented Old De Lacey as blind and this was important to two of the novel's key themes. Unlike the rest of the family, Old De Lacey is able to respond sympathetically to the monster. This allowed Shelley to illustrate the themes of exclusion and prejudice.

Now rewrite it using the **present tense** consistently:

....

....

....

....

....

PROGRESS LOG [tick the correct box]   Needs more work ☐   Getting there ☐   Under control ☐

Tackling exam tasks (A01) (A02)

DECODING QUESTIONS

It is important to be able to identify key words in exam tasks and then quickly generate some ideas.

❶ Read this task and notice how the **key words** have been underlined.

Read Volume Two, Chapter VI.

Question: *In what ways does <u>Shelley</u> <u>present</u> the <u>monster</u> as a <u>sympathetic</u> figure*

- *in this <u>chapter</u>*
- *in the <u>novel as a whole?</u>*

Now do the same with this task, i.e. underline the key words:

Read Volume Three, Chapter VI.

Question: *Explain how Shelley explores the theme of isolation*

- *in this chapter*
- *in the novel as a whole.*

GENERATING IDEAS

❷ Now you need to generate ideas quickly. Use the spider-diagram* below and add as many ideas of your own as you can:

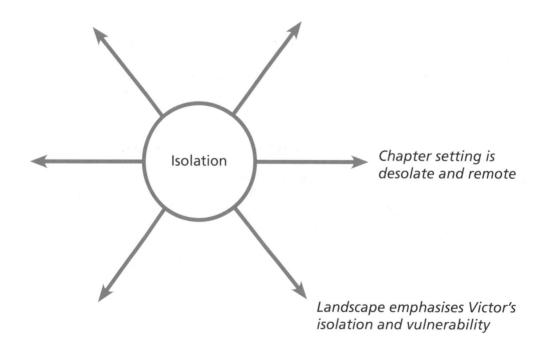

*You can do this as a list if you wish.

PLANNING AN ESSAY

Here is the **exam-style** task from the previous page:

Read Volume Three, Chapter VI.

Question: *Explain how Shelley explores the theme of isolation*

- *in this chapter*
- *in the novel as a whole.*

❸ **Using the ideas you generated,** write a simple **plan** including at least **five key points** (the first two have been done for you). Check back to your spider diagram or the list you made.

a) *Victor and the monster are isolated in a very desolate and remote landscape in this chapter.*

b) *The landscape emphasises Victor's solitude and vulnerability as he meets the monster.*

c) ....

....

d) ....

....

e) ....

....

❹ Now list **five quotations**, one for each point (the first two have been provided for you):

a) *'mountains of ice, which admit of no escape'*

b) *'He bounded over the crevices in the ice, among which I had walked with caution'*

c) ....

....

d) ....

....

e) ....

....

❺ Now read this task and **write a plan of your own,** including **quotations**, on a separate sheet of paper.

Read Volume Two, Chapter I.

Question: *Explain how Shelley presents Victor as an outcast from society*

- *in this chapter*
- *in the novel as a whole.*

PROGRESS LOG [tick the correct box]   Needs more work ☐   Getting there ☐   Under control ☐

Sample answers (A01) (A02) (A03) (A04)*

OPENING PARAGRAPHS

Read Volume Two, Chapter II.

Question: *Explain how Shelley explores the theme of isolation*

- *in this chapter*

- *in the novel as a whole.*

Now look at these two alternate openings to the essay and read the examiner comments underneath:

Student A

> *Victor does not start off isolated in Shelley's 'Frankenstein' because he has a loving family. However, when he creates the monster he has to hide because of his guilt. Shelley carries on with this theme through the monster, because the monster is also an outcast. Society drives the monster away because of how he looks. Victor is driven away by his own guilt and fear.*

Student B

> *In this chapter, Shelley's description of the 'terrifically desolate' landscape highlights the theme of isolation. Victor's actions have driven him to this remote setting. There is also a feeling that he is trapped here because the mountains 'admit of no escape'. This suggests that the monster might pose a threat to Victor, which he later does.*

Expert viewpoint 1: This paragraph correctly identifies the thematic importance of the isolation of Victor and his monster, and relates this to Victor's guilt over the creation of his monster. However, the response fails to state what else the essay will cover, or refer to the extract in the question.

Expert viewpoint 2: This is quite well-written and the student makes valid inferences as to how the description of the landscapes relates to the theme. It could be made clearer, though, that the monster is also an isolated figure in this landscape and that he becomes more isolated later in the text.

❶ Which comment belongs to which answer? Match the paragraph (A or B) to the expert's feedback (1 or 2).

Student A: .... Student B: ....

❷ Now write the opening paragraph to this task on a separate sheet of paper:

Explain how Shelley deals with the themes of prejudice and guilt

- *in this chapter*

- *in the novel as a whole.*

Remember:

- Introduce the topic in general terms, perhaps **explaining** or **'unpicking'** the key **words** or **ideas** in the task (such as 'explore').

- Mention the **different possibilities** or ideas that you are going to address.

- Use the **author's name.**

*AO4 is assessed by OCR only.

WRITING ABOUT TECHNIQUES

Here are two paragraphs in response to a different task, where the students have focused on the writer's techniques. The task is:

Read Volume Two, Chapter II.

Question: *Explain how Shelley creates sympathy for the monster*

- *in this chapter*
- *in the novel as a whole.*

Student A

The monster's speech here is eloquent, dignified and moving. The monster is shown to be intelligent and articulate, and to have many other human qualities. The monster, for instance, recognises Victor's selfishness in creating and abandoning him; he challenges Victor with the words, 'How dare you sport thus with life?' The use of the word 'sport' illustrates that Victor's attitude towards the creation of new life has been careless and arrogant. This is the first of Shelley's highly sympathetic portrayals of the monster and it foreshadows the monster's own account of his tragic life later in the text.

Student B

Shelley shows the reader that, although the monster is hideous in appearance, he has a human-like identity. There are things about the monster that make the reader relate to him. At first, Victor wants to kill his creation, but Victor himself then feels sorry for the monster like the reader does. By showing us this meeting, Shelley gives the reader a different point of view on the monster and lets the reader experience sympathy for the creature. This paves the way for the monster to be seen as more and more sympathetic when he tells the reader more about himself later on.

Expert viewpoint 1: This mid-level response highlights accurately how the monster's conversation with Victor elicits the reader's sympathy, but does not focus in detail on the techniques used by Shelley to achieve this – specifically, the language that she attributes to the monster and the particular human qualities he demonstrates here. It is also a little awkward in its expression and limited in its vocabulary.

Mid level

Expert viewpoint 2: This high-level response comments on the specific techniques used by Shelley to generate a sympathetic portrayal of the monster and draws accurate inferences concerning the qualities that might be attributed to the monster. It gives a relevant direct quotation to illustrate a key point, zooms in appropriately on a key word, and relates the material in this chapter to later relevant developments in the novel.

High level

❸ Which comment belongs to which answer? Match the paragraph (A or B) to the expert's feedback (1 or 2).

Student A: ....   Student B: ....

❹ Now take another **episode** from the novel which shows the monster in a sympathetic light and on a separate sheet of paper write your own **paragraph**. You could **comment** on:

- The monster's account of the De Laceys
- The monster's meeting with Walton at the very end of the novel

Read this **lower-level** response to the following task:

Read Volume One, Letter I.

Question: *Explain how Shelley explores the theme of ambition*

- *in this opening letter*
- *elsewhere in the novel.*

Student response

Walton is really excited here about his trip and he shows his ambitions by telling his sister what he hopes to find out about the region and its secrets. He is a brave man and talks about his 'enthusiasm' even though the trip is going to be dangerous. You could say he is foolish for not thinking it through.

Walton is a bit like Victor because of this and later on he sympathises with Victor.

Expert viewpoint: The response correctly identifies the nature of Walton's ambition and his enthusiasm for scientific discovery, although it does so in vague terms and the one-word quotation should be supported with further evidence from the text. The student is right to comment on Walton's appreciation of the danger of the trip, and on the similarity between Walton and Victor which Shelley develops later. However, the comments are rather vague and the expression is quite simplistic and informal, for instance 'you could say …', 'a bit like …' and so on.

⑤ **Rewrite** these two **paragraphs** in your own words, improving them by addressing:

- The lack of development of linking of points – no **'zooming in'** on **key words and phrases**
- The lack of **quotations and embedding**
- Unnecessary **repetition**, poor **specialist terms** and use of **vocabulary**

Paragraph 1:

In this extract, Shelley presents Walton ....

....

However, it is clear that Walton ....

....

and this implies that ....

....

....

....

Paragraph 2:

This idea is developed later in the novel when ....

....

and it becomes clear that ....

....

....

....

A FULL-LENGTH RESPONSE

⑥ Write a **full-length response** to this exam-style task on a separate sheet of paper.
Answer both parts of the question:

Read Volume One, Letter IV.

Question: *Explain how Victor is presented as a sympathetic figure*

- *in this extract*
- *in the novel as a whole.*

Remember to do the following:

- Plan **quickly** (no more than five minutes) what you intend to write, jotting down **four or five supporting quotations**.
- Refer closely to the **key words** in the question.
- Make sure you comment on **what** Shelley does, the **techniques** she uses and the **effect** of those techniques.
- Support your points with **well-chosen quotations** or other evidence.
- Develop your points by **'zooming in'** on particular **words** or **phrases** and explaining their **effect**.
- Be **persuasive** and **convincing** in what you say.
- Check carefully for **spelling**, **punctuation** and **grammar**.

PROGRESS LOG [tick the correct box]   Needs more work ☐   Getting there ☐   Under control ☐

Further questions

❶ How is Victor presented as a tragic figure in the final volume of the novel?

❷ What is significant about the fate of Justine? Think about:

- The theme of justice
- The representation of women

❸ In what ways does the novel criticise excessive ambition?

❹ How important is the character of Walton to the novel?

❺ What is the significance of the fact that Victor destroys the monster's female companion in Volume Three, Chapter III?

❻ How does Shelley portray the monster as a tragic figure in his first-person account of his experiences in Volume Two?

PROGRESS LOG [tick the correct box]   Needs more work ☐   Getting there ☐   Under control ☐

Note: Answers have been provided for most tasks. Exceptions are 'Practice tasks' and tasks which ask you to write a paragraph or use your own words or judgement.

PART TWO: PLOT AND ACTION

Volume One, Letter I [pp. 8–9]

1 a) F; b) F; c) T; d) T; e) F; f) T; g) F

2 a) He describes the Arctic as an unknown region full of secrets to be uncovered and this excites his ambition. He feels his heart 'glow' (p. 16) with enthusiasm.

b) He is excited by the prospect of visiting a dramatic, unchartered region which he imagines as a place of 'beauty and delight' (p. 15).

c) Walton confides his feelings in his sister. He calls her 'dear Margaret' (p. 17), and signs himself 'your affectionate brother' (p. 18).

3

Point/detail	Evidence	Effect or explanation
1: *Walton is an ambitious man.*	'I preferred glory to every enticement'	He seeks above all else to make a name for himself.
2: *He has a sense of responsibility for others.*	'I am required … to raise the spirits of others'	Walton is a strong leader who will seek to motivate others.
3: *He is a courageous man.*	'My courage and my resolution is firm'	Walton has some heroic qualities which later help him sympathise with Victor's courage and ambition.

Volume One, Letters II–III [pp. 10–11]

1 a) dauntless courage; b) 'desirous of glory'; c) *The Ancient Mariner*; d) bad weather; e) icebergs

2 a) The master gave away his inheritance to enable the woman he loved to marry her beloved.

b) He wants someone to confide in.

c) Large sheets of ice suggest the dangers of the region the ship is bound for.

3

Point/detail	Evidence	Effect or explanation
1: *Walton is a sociable man.*	'I greatly feel the want of a friend.'	Walton feels isolated and this depresses him, making him more welcoming of Victor later on.
2: *Shelley sets up a comparison between Walton and the ship's lieutenant.*	The lieutenant 'is madly desirous of glory'.	Both men are ambitious, and the word 'madly' suggests their ambition might be excessive.
3: *Walton has a gentle, compassionate temperament.*	'I cannot overcome an intense distaste to the usual brutality exercised on board ship'	Walton is unusually sensitive for a sea captain which makes him vulnerable later, when the crew begin to rebel.

Volume One, Letter IV [pp. 12–13]

1 a) F; b) T; c) F; d) F; e) T; f) T

2 a) He is a man of 'gigantic stature' (p. 25) which makes him seem not quite human.

b) Victor has clearly been through a dreadful ordeal which has wrecked his health. He refers to his terrible 'fate' (p. 31) and promises to tell Walton his story.

c) Walton immediately feels sympathy for and curiosity about Victor. The reader shares Walton's perspective.

3

Point/detail	Evidence	Effect or explanation
1: *The monster is presented as something intriguing, almost like a wild beast or creature.*	'This appearance excited our unqualified wonder.'	The figure appears almost inhuman and somewhat threatening.
2: *Victor appears to be an educated foreigner.*	'the stranger addressed me in English, although with a foreign accent.'	This excites Walton's, and the reader's, curiosity.
3: *Victor is in a dangerous physical condition.*	'a man on the brink of destruction'	Shelley suggests Victor is near death. Her choice of the word 'destruction' is ironic given Victor's pursuit of creation.

Volume One, Chapter I [pp. 14–15]

1 We learn that Victor's family are **Swiss** by nationality, although Victor was born in **Naples**. His father is called **Alphonse** and his mother **Caroline**. A girl named **Elizabeth** is **adopted** by Victor's parents. She is an **orphan** from a **poor/peasant** family. Victor describes his childhood as 'but one train of **enjoyment** to me'.

2 a) Victor describes his upbringing as shaped by the kind, nurturing qualities of his parents. They also show their compassion in adopting Elizabeth.

b) Victor regarded Elizabeth from the outset as a beautiful and virtuous girl. He develops a very strong affection for her.

c) Elizabeth's father was a decent, but rather reckless man. Although courageous, he lacked the good sense of Alphonse and was not a reliable or wise parent.

3

Point/detail	Evidence	Effect or explanation
1: *Victor has a strong sense of Elizabeth's virtue.*	She is 'heaven-sent'.	He describes her as an angelic creature, hinting at the strength of his feelings for her.
2: *Victor notices that Elizabeth seems different from her foster parents.*	'appeared of a different stock.'	Elizabeth seems to share the class background of Victor's family, and not that of her foster parents.
3: *Elizabeth, like her real father, is portrayed as a courageous character.*	'exerted himself to obtain the liberty of his country.'	Her father acted on behalf of others, and later we see Elizabeth's own courage when she defends Justine.

Volume One, Chapter II [pp. 16–17]

1 a) closest friend; b) alchemy; c) Geneva; d) 'sad trash'; e) a lightning strike

2 a) Victor and Henry are both very passionate men with a lively imagination. They also share a deep love of nature.

b) Victor avidly reads the work of old scientists and philosophers. He describes his passion as welling up 'like a mountain river' (p. 40).

c) He is inspired and fascinated by the natural world. He seeks to 'penetrate' (p. 41) its mysteries.

3

Point/detail	Evidence	Effect or explanation
1: Victor regards nature with great scientific curiosity.	'The world was to me a secret which I desired to divine.'	The word 'secret' suggests that the knowledge Victor seeks is a hidden truth, and possibly even a forbidden knowledge.
2: Elizabeth has a different temperament from Victor.	'Elizabeth was of a calmer and more concentrated disposition'	Victor is more impulsive and temperamental. He sees that Elizabeth has a calming influence over him.
3: Victor is something of a loner.	'It was my temper to avoid a crowd'	This prepares us for Victor's self-imposed isolation later in the novel.

Volume One, Chapters III–V [pp. 18–19]

1 a) T; b) F; c) F; d) F; e) T; f) T

2 a) He refers to her as 'the best of women' (Ch. III, p. 45) and is devastated by her death.

b) Victor isolates himself completely and his behaviour becomes increasingly eratic. He responds to the monster with horror and uses violent, Gothic images to describe his creation.

c) It is clear that Victor's earlier hopes of creating a creature more beautiful than any man have perished. His creation repulses him and he turns his back on it.

3

Point/detail	Evidence	Effect or explanation
1: Victor does not sleep easily after the monster's creation.	'I was disturbed by the wildest dreams.'	Victor's imagination has been profoundly unsettled by the sight of the monster.
2: Victor's dream connects Elizabeth with his mother.	'her features appeared to change, and I thought that I held the corpse of my dead mother'	Victor sees Elizabeth as a protective mother-figure. The death of his mother anticipates the later death of Elizabeth.
3: Victor awakes to find the monster by his bed.	'I beheld the wretch – the miserable monster'	The sight of the monster straight after the dream anticipates the threat posed by the monster later on.

Volume One, Chapters VI–VII [pp. 20–1]

1 Victor receives a letter from **Elizabeth** which informs him of the return of **Justine** to the family after some time away. Victor introduces **Henry** to his professors at the university in **Ingolstad**. In Chapter VII, Victor learns from **Alphonse** about the death of **William**. He makes his way back to **Geneva**. During the journey, Victor catches a glimpse of the **monster**. The chapter ends with Justine accused of William's **murder**.

2 a) Justine is a very kind, sweet-tempered girl. She works as a servant for the family and is much loved by them.

b) The landscape is dramatic and desolate. Its power is linked to that of the monster who appears illuminated by lightning.

c) Shelley introduces the themes of violent crime and the justice system through William's murder.

3

Point/detail	Evidence	Effect or explanation
1: Victor's Romantic temperament is demonstrated by his response to the outbreak of a storm.	'This noble war in the sky elevated my spirits.'	This shows the sublime power of nature, but is also a reminder of Victor's – and mankind's – weakness in the face of natural forces.
2: Victor responds with horror to the glimpse of the monster.	'it was the wretch, the filthy daemon to whom I had given life.'	The monster is portrayed as evil and Victor remains horrified by his role in its creation.
3: Victor believes the monster killed William.	'He was the murderer! I could not doubt it.'	Victor attributes a capacity for criminal violence to the monster, and his intuition is correct.

Volume One, Chapter VIII [pp. 22–3]

1 a) created the monster; b) a miniature portrait of Caroline; c) Elizabeth; d) a priest; e) hostility; f) to be hanged

2 a) Elizabeth is shown to have a strong sense of justice and to be courageous in defence of Justine.

b) The reader knows that Justine is innocent. The criminal system is shown as incompetent and hostile to her, convicting her on the basis of a false confession.

c) Victor is devastated by the death of the virtuous, innocent woman. He feels responsible for her fate because he created the monster.

3

Point/detail	Evidence	Effect or explanation
1: Justine's religion is a comfort to her.	'God raises my weakness and gives me courage to endure the worst.'	Justine retains her dignity and faith, which enhances her virtue and strengthens Shelley's exploration of the justice system.
2: Victor is thrown into deep despair.	'where I could conceal the horrid anguish that possessed me.'	Victor feels not only grief, but guilt at Justine's wrongful conviction for murder.
3: Victor describes Justine in spiritual terms.	'the saintly sufferer'	Justine's goodness and courage render her execution all the more horrific to the reader.

Volume Two, Chapter I [pp. 24–5]

1 a) commit suicide; b) 'fiend'; c) two; d) nobody

2 a) Victor describes his creation as a 'fiend' (p. 94) and himself as an 'evil spirit' (p. 93) which shows that he sees a connection between the monster and himself. He describes himself as being in 'hell' (p. 93) on account of his guilty secret.

b) Victor hides away out of guilt. The desolation of the mountains reflects his state of mind and links him to the monster.

c) Victor describes his wish to avenge the deaths of William and Justine and to prevent further killings.

3

Point/detail	Evidence	Effect or explanation
1: *Victor decides against suicide for the sake of his loved ones.*	He cannot 'leave them exposed and unprotected to the malice of the fiend'.	*Victor feels responsible for what the monster might do next and guilty for having created this threat to his family.*
2: *Victor uses Gothic imagery to describe his despair.*	'the dark cloud which brooded over me.'	*This imagery creates suspense and terror in relation to Victor's fate.*
3: *Victor feels he must avoid society.*	'I shunned the face of man'	*Victor's self-imposed isolation increases his sense of despair and guilt.*

Volume Two, Chapter II [pp. 26–7]

1 a) T; b) F; c) T; d) F; e) T; f) F

2 a) The monster describes his suffering very eloquently. The reader understands the pain caused by Victor's abandonment of his creation.

b) The dramatic, isolated region adds drama to the encounter and emphasises the isolation of Victor and the monster.

c) The monster has a sense of justice in that he sees how Victor has wronged him. He shows also an ability to feel great emotional pain.

3

Point/detail	Evidence	Effect or explanation
1: *The monster describes his isolation.*	'Everywhere I see bliss, from which I alone am irrevocably excluded.'	*The monster regards himself as an outcast and is deeply distressed.*
2: *The monster begs Victor for better treatment.*	'Make me happy, and I shall again be virtuous.'	*The monster wants Victor to treat him as a good father would, and suggests his violent behaviour is due to Victor's ill-treatment of him.*
3: *The monster condemns Victor for having created him.*	'How dare you sport thus with life?'	*The monster accuses Victor of irresponsibly 'playing God' with his creation.*

Volume Two, Chapter III [pp. 28–9]

1 *The monster describes resting in a forest close to* **Ingolstad**. *He describes seeing the light of the* **moon** *and listening to the* **birds**. *He then travels to a village where the locals* **attack** *him. The monster finds shelter in a* **hovel** *by a cottage. He hears an old* **man** *playing music and is entranced by it. He observes the family's distress and feels* **sorrow**.

2 a) He says that everything seemed 'confused and indistinct' (p. 104). He feels strong sensations, but cannot understand them.

b) The villagers are terrified by the appearance of the monster and are violent towards him. This deepens the monster's sense of his own differences and lessens his trust in humanity.

c) The monster's sensitive, intelligent reaction to the music shows the reader that the monster has human qualities and perceptions.

3

Point/detail	Evidence	Effect or explanation
1: *Shelley describes the monster's pleasurable response to Old De Lacey's music.*	'sounds sweeter than the voice of the thrush or the nightingale.'	*Shelley uses the alliteration of 'sounds sweeter' to express the sensory pleasure the monster finds in music.*
2: *The monster's language conveys the complexity and strangeness of his new experiences.*	'A strange multiplicity of sensations seized me and I saw, felt, heard, and smelt at the same time'	The first-person narrative captures the overwhelming intensity of the monster's sensations.
3: *The monster's description of Old De Lacey shows that he believes the man to be kind, yet vulnerable.*	'The silver hair and benevolent countenance of the aged cottager'	*The adjectives show that the monster appreciates Old De Lacey's advanced age and good nature.*

Volume Two, Chapter IV [pp. 30–1]

1 a) De Lacey; b) blind; c) speak; d) 'this miserable deformity'; e) Agatha; f) collecting firewood

2 a) He feels immediate sympathy for the De Laceys even though he has no education and no experience of human society.

b) The De Laceys are very poor, but also virtuous and proud people. Their cottage is bare, but clean and homely.

c) Old De Lacey's children show great kindness and respect to their father. The monster is deeply moved by this.

3

Point/detail	Evidence	Effect or explanation
1: *The monster sees his reflection and responds with despair.*	'I was in reality the monster that I am, I was filled with the bitterest sensations'	*The monster sees himself as monstrous and feels excluded from the De Laceys.*
2: *The monster acts to help the family.*	'I … collected my own food and fuel for the cottage.'	*This shows his natural benevolence in seeking to help the impoverished family.*
3: *The monster becomes more curious about human society.*	'I longed to discover the motives and feelings of these lovely creatures;'	*Shelley shows how the monster wishes to understand human society, and also to fit into it himself.*

Volume Two, Chapters V–VI [pp. 32–3]

1 a) F; b) T; c) T; d) F; e) T; f) T

2 a) The monster is deeply moved when he sees how warmly the family welcome Safie.

b) The whole family was banished from France because of Felix's role in helping Safie's father escape.

c) The monster's curiosity about the De Lacey family makes him wonder about his own parentage. He asks, 'What was I?' (Ch. V, p. 124).

ANSWERS

3

Point/detail	Evidence	Effect or explanation
1: *The monster questions his identity.*	*'What was I?'*	*He becomes aware of his difference from other humans and his questions fuel his desire to learn more about his origins.*
2: *The monster learns that humans can be cruel.*	*'Was man, indeed, at once so powerful, so virtuous, and magnificent, yet so vicious and base?'*	*The monster understands more about humankind through hearing about the De Laceys' troubled history.*
3: *The monster wishes he had remained isolated.*	*'Oh, that I had forever remained in my native wood'*	*He becomes increasingly aware of and pained by his exclusion from human society.*

Volume Two, Chapters VII–IX (pp. 34–5)

1 *The monster learns to **read** by collecting three books, which are **Paradise** Lost, Lives and Sorrows of **Werter**. By reading **Victor's / Frankenstein's** journal he learns about his own **origin**.*

*He visits Old De Lacey who cannot see how the monster looks because he is **blind**. The old man treats the monster with **kindness**. The rest of the family, however, are appalled by his appearance and react by **chasing** him away. They then leave their home and the monster **burns** down the cottage. He goes to **Geneva** where he kills William. The monster then meets Victor and asks him to create a **female**. Victor eventually **agrees** because he is **moved** by the monster's plight.*

2 a) He is appalled by the circumstances of his creation, but tries not to despair.

b) The monster wants to experience the comfort and joy of human love. This was something he observed through his encounter with the De Laceys.

c) Victor suffers agonies of despair when the monster leaves him, and wishes he could 'become as nought' (Ch. IX, p. 151).

3

Point/detail	Evidence	Effect or explanation
1: *The monster's tale has the effect of Victor wanting to offer comfort to him, something which will have long-term implications.*	*'I was moved.'*	*Victor feels some sympathy for his creation and guilt for abandoning him.*
2: *The monster threatens violence if Victor does not meet his demands.*	*'I will work at your destruction'*	*This anticipates the later events of the novel and shows the monster's capacity for vengeance.*
3: *The monster seeks a companion.*	*'I demand a creature of another sex.'*	*The monster craves a female mate and insists that Victor provide such a companion, as God created Eve for Adam.*

Volume Three, Chapter I [pp. 36–7]

1 a) T; b) F; c) T; d) T; e) F; f) T

2 a) Alphonse wrongly believes that Victor has fallen in love with another woman. He thinks that this is the cause of Victor's despair.

b) As Victor contemplates the task, he begins to feel 'repugnance' (p. 155) towards it. However, he fears the monster's vengeance if he does not comply.

c) Clerval is a deeply imaginative, passionate man with a strong appreciation of nature and a more stable temperament than Victor.

3

Point/detail	Evidence	Effect or explanation
1: *Like Victor, Clerval is characterised as a typical Romantic figure.*	*'His wild and enthusiastic imagination'*	*The idea of wildness suggests something uncontrolled, which links him to Victor.*
2: *Clerval's nature is kind and affectionate.*	*'His soul overflowed with ardent affections'*	*Shelley uses the metaphor of overflowing water to describe Clerval's friendship and to link him with nature.*
3: *There is a suggestion that something terrible has happened to Clerval.*	*'Is this gentle and lovely being lost forever?'*	*The reader anticipates that Clerval may have been killed by the monster by the time that Victor comes to narrate his story.*

Volume Three, Chapters II–III [pp. 38–9]

1 *Victor and Clerval stay in London until **March** when they travel to **Edinburgh**. They pass through **Windsor** and Oxford, and then **Matlock** and the Lake District before reaching Scotland. Victor then retires to the remote location of **Orkney** in order to create the monster's **mate**. In Chapter III, Victor decides to **destroy** the female creation and the **monster** watches him do this. The monster vows to be with Victor on his **wedding** night. Victor sets sail and arrives in **Ireland** where he is arrested for **murder**.*

2 a) The Lake District connects the novel to the context of the Romantic movement. Many of the Romantic poets visited or lived in the Lake District.

b) Victor imagines that his second creation might be more monstrous than this first. He fears they might reproduce and create a race like themselves.

c) The monster reacts with fury and vows to take revenge on Victor.

3

Point/detail	Evidence	Effect or explanation
1: *Victor begins to contemplate the consequences of his actions, and to change his mind.*	*'a train of reflection occurred to me, which led me to consider the effects'*	*Victor realises that the consequences of his actions could be disastrous.*
2: *Victor has fears that a female monster might be even more destructive than the male.*	*'she might become ten thousand times more malignant than her mate'*	*Victor fears the terrible consequences for himself and humanity if he creates a female version of the monster.*
3: *Victor fears the two monsters might reproduce.*	*'A race of devils would be propagated upon the earth'*	*This conveys the sense that the monsters could only produce evil, hellish offspring and highlights the theme of unnatural creation.*

Volume Three, Chapter IV [pp. 40–1]

1, 2 violence (p. 179); prejudice (p. 180); justice system (p. 186); isolation (p. 182); revenge (p. 181)

3 a) Justine was wrongly accused of the murder of William and here Victor is wrongly suspected of killing Clerval. The monster is the murderer in both cases.

b) Victor almost faints when he sees the corpse of Clerval, which the magistrate takes as a sign of guilt.

c) Alphonse is again represented as a loving, responsible father. He supports Victor in prison and then takes him home.

4

Point/detail	Evidence	Effect or explanation
1: Victor is initially optimistic about the outcome of the legal proceedings.	'I was perfectly tranquil as to the consequences of the affair.'	Victor's word 'tranquil' is reassuring but Shelley may hint at false optimism here, given the likely outcome.
2: Victor realises that the monster has killed Henry.	'Have my murderous machinations deprived you also, my dearest Henry, of life?'	His rhetorical question emphasises his despair at having made his best friend the third victim of the monster's revenge.
3: Victor becomes dangerously ill after seeing the body.	'I lay for two months on the point of death'	The use of first-person narration to describe his physical and mental breakdown heightens the drama.

Volume Three, Chapters V–VI [pp. 42–3]

1 a) T; **b)** F; **c)** F; **d)** T; **e)** T; **f)** T; **g)** F

2 a) We know that the monster has vowed to be with Victor on his wedding night. Victor also dreamed of Elizabeth's death the night after creating the monster.

b) The monster wishes to destroy Victor's mate, just as Victor destroyed the monster's.

c) Shelley uses pathetic fallacy to link the violence of the storm to the violence threatening Victor and Elizabeth.

3

Point/detail	Evidence	Effect or explanation
1: Shelley presents the murder from Victor's perspective. He hears a scream and realises Elizabeth is in danger.	'As I heard it, the whole truth rushed into my mind'	Shelley conveys, through Victor's sudden understanding, that Elizabeth is the monster's target, and not Victor himself.
2: Elizabeth is presented as a blameless victim of the monster through Victor's description of her virtue.	'the destruction of the best hope, and the purest creature of earth?'	The goodness and purity associated with Elizabeth intensifies the horror of her violent death.
3: Shelley presents clear physical evidence that the monster is the murderer.	'The murderous mark of the fiend's grasp was on her neck'	This mark of the monster's violence is present on all the murder victims, and is immediately recognised by Victor.

Volume Three, Chapter VII [pp. 44–5]

1 a) call on spirits to help him; **b)** laugh; **c)** the Arctic; **d)** Walton; **e)** destroy the monster; **f)** commit suicide

2 a) Victor has lost the people closest to him and is in total despair. He accepts that his ambition to create life has had tragic consequences.

b) The Arctic is the most desolate and inhospitable of all the novel's locations. It reflects Victor's and the monster's complete alienation from human society at the end of the novel.

c) The monster has suffered greatly because of Victor's actions in creating him, and then refusing to care for him. The monster feels himself to be a worthless 'wretch' (p. 224) who has murdered innocent people and now deserves to die.

3

Point/detail	Evidence	Effect or explanation
1: Themes of vengeance and death are emphasised in the heightened language Victor uses.	'swear that he shall not live'	Victor's desire for vengeance remains and reveals his continued loathing for the monster.
2: Victor uses the satanic imagery of Gothic horror fiction to portray the monster as wicked.	'His soul is as hellish as his form'	Victor sees the monster as inherently and irredeemably wicked.
3: Walton's use of violent Gothic imagery conveys to his sister the horror of Victor's tale.	'do you not feel your blood congeal with horror'	Margaret stands in the position of the reader here, who is also expected to be horrified by this tale.

PART THREE: CHARACTERS

Who's who? [p. 47]

1 Robert Walton; Victor Frankenstein; The monster; Elizabeth Lavenza/Frankenstein; Justine Moritz; Henry Clerval; Old De Lacey; William Frankenstein

The characters missing are:

The Frankenstein family	The De Lacey family	The tutors at Ingolstad	Others?
Alphonse	Felix	M. Waldman	Safie
Caroline	Agatha	M. Krempe	Mr Kirwin, magistrate
Ernest			

Robert Walton [p. 48]

1 a) T; **b)** F; **c)** T; **d)** T; **e)** NEE; **f)** T; **g)** F

2 a) of bad weather.

b) Victor is an educated, sensitive and brave man.

c) he resolves to pursue his project to the Arctic in spite of the dangers.

e) he is too focused on his ambition.

f) their Romantic temperament, their ambition, their determination.

ANSWERS

Victor Frankenstein [p. 49]

1 a) 1: Alchemy; 2: Nature

b) 1: Hope that the monster will be a glorious creation; 2: Horror at the reality of the monster's appearance

c) 1: Anger; 2: Sympathy

2

Evidence	For	Against
He is motivated to create the monster by the prospect of glory.	✓	
Victor insists on telling his story truthfully to Walton.	✓	✓
His immediate response to the monster is one of revulsion and he abandons his creation.	✓	
Victor agrees to create a companion for the monster.		✓
Victor feels responsible for the deaths of William and Justine.		✓
Victor feels guilt and fear after creating the monster and hides himself away.	✓	✓

Alphonse [p. 50]

1 a) husband; b) father; c) adoptive father; d) friend; e) father

2 *Alphonse marries the daughter of his friend* **Beaufort**. *His first-born son is called* **Victor** *and he hopes to see his eldest son marry* **Elizabeth** *who is Alphonse and Caroline's* **adopted** *daughter. Alphonse is very dismissive of Victor's interest in* **alchemy**, *although he does not explain why. He is also very protective of Victor, coming to his aid when Victor is accused of killing* **Clerval**. *Alphonse dies shortly after the death of* **Elizabeth**.

Elizabeth [p. 51]

1 nurturing; gentle; chaste; just; passive; honest

2 a) 1: He describes her as having quite angelic qualities. 2: He describes her as the 'best' (Vol. Three, Ch. VI, p. 199) of women following her death.

b) 1: She has democratic values. 2: She defends the innocence of Justine.

c) 1: She becomes a mother-figure to Victor's brothers. 2: She shows great loyalty to Justine.

The monster [p. 52]

1 a) gigantic; b) superhuman; c) blind; d) Justine; e) female; f) Elizabeth; g) the Arctic

Henry Clerval, William Frankenstein, Old De Lacey [p. 53]

Quotation	Henry	William	Old De Lacey
'of singular talent and fancy'	✓		
'laughing blue eyes, dark eyelashes, and curling hair'		✓	
'descended from a good family in France'			✓

2 a) Victor describes Henry as warm and passionate, with a 'wild and enthusiastic imagination' (Vol. Three, Ch. I, p. 161). Victor also describes the trips that he takes with Henry and the reader learns of Henry's great sensitivity to the natural world which resembles that of the Romantic poets of Shelley's time.

b) Victor's youngest brother William is murdered by the monster in the first of his acts of revenge against Victor. The monster frames

Justine for the murder and she is executed for it, which plunges Victor into even greater despair as he holds himself responsible for both deaths.

c) Both Old De Lacey and Alphonse are ideal father-figures in terms of their paternal benevolence, wisdom and support of their children. In terms of the novel's wider themes, they can be contrasted in this with Victor's callous abandonment of his 'son', the monster.

3 a) Old De Lacey; b) Henry Clerval; c) William

Caroline Beaufort, Justine Moritz, Safie [p. 54]

1 a) Alphonse; b) Elizabeth; c) Frankenstein; d) William; e) Turkish; f) Felix De Lacey

2

	Caroline	Justine	Safie
a servant		✓	
loyal	✓	✓	✓
compassionate	✓	✓	✓
honest	✓	✓	✓
married	✓		
a mother	✓		
courageous	✓	✓	✓
proud			
gentle	✓	✓	✓
ambitious			
wealthy			

PART FOUR: THEMES, CONTEXTS AND SETTINGS

Themes [pp. 56–9]

1 Probable choices are: revenge; ambition; knowledge; isolation; nature; Romanticism; justice; prejudice

Possible choices might be: love; power; companionship

2 a) revenge; ambition; knowledge; isolation; prejudice

b) Romanticism; nature; love; companionship

c) revenge; prejudice

d) justice; prejudice

e) love; justice; companionship

f) ambition; isolation

g) prejudice

3 a) Walton is a highly ambitious man with a passionate temperament and what he seeks above all else is knowledge about the regions he intends to visit on his expedition. Victor likewise is passionate about the uncovering the secrets of natural world and both men become blind to the negative consequences of their ambitious projects.

b) Both Victor and his monster are increasingly isolated from human society as the novel progresses and suffer the pain of exclusion and unjust treatment. They are also motivated to seek revenge against one another.

4 a) The monster's exclusion from and rejection by the De Lacey family

b) Victor's self-imposed isolation after he creates the monster

c) Walton's isolation as he journeys north

6 a) they assume she is guilty

b) he is horrified at what he has created

c) they are horrified by his appearance

d) the French legal system is prejudiced against the Turkish foreigner

8

Point/detail	Evidence	Effect or explanation
1: *The monster's suffering highlights Victor's injustice.*	*'be not equitable to every other, and trample upon me alone, to whom thy justice, and even thy clemency and affection, is most due.'*	*The monster appeals directly to Victor's sense of justice as the creator of a being that deserves the compassion due from a father to a child.*
2: *The monster believes Victor should make amends.*	*'Remember that I am thy creature, I ought to be thy Adam.'*	*The monster compares Victor to God who created Adam, and asks for the justice owed to him as Victor's creation.*
3: *The monster seeks Victor's love.*	*'to whom thy justice, and even thy clemency and affection, is most due.'*	*Even though the creature is monstrous in appearance, he appeals for the love a creator should feel for his 'son'.*

Contexts [pp. 60–1]

1 a) William Godwin; b) Percy; c) Galvani; d) Prometheus; e) *Paradise Lost*; f) Romanticism; g) *Faust*; h) Geneva

2 a) Scientists were investigating the origin of various natural forces, including electricity. Galvani carried out experiments which involved passing currents through matter and this inspired Shelley in describing how Frankenstein creates the monster.

b) Prometheus is a figure from Greek myth who stole fire from the gods and was punished for his pride and ambition. Victor likewise seeks to uncover the hidden secrets of nature and his transgression leads to his downfall.

c) Shelley quotes Milton's poem *Paradise Lost* at the start of *Frankenstein* and in the quotation, Adam asks God why he was created only then to be cast out of Eden. The monster refers to himself as 'Adam' and asks Victor why he was created only then to be abandoned and to fall into sin.

3 a) 'The beauty of the dream vanished, and breathless horror filled my heart' (Vol. One, Ch. V, p. 58)

b) 'I, like the archfiend, bore a hell within me' (Vol. Two, Ch. 8, p. 138)

c) 'Ruined castles hanging on the precipices of piny mountains' (Vol. Two, Ch. I, p. 97)

Settings [pp. 62–3]

1 The Arctic; Evian; Irish Prison; The Orkney Islands; De Lacey Cottage; The Alps; Ingolstadt; Belrive, Geneva

2 a) The monster meets Victor.

b) Victor goes to university.

c) Victor is imprisoned on suspicion of murder.

3 a) The sublime was an important concept in the Romantic period that referred to the grandeur of natural settings, and Shelley describes the Alps in terms of their enormity, magnificence and power. The landscape is 'immense', 'magnificent' (Vol. Two, Ch. I, p. 97) and 'terrifically desolate' (Vol. Two, Ch. II, p. 100).

b) Walton's journey to the Arctic highlights the importance of acquiring knowledge through the exploration of the natural world, and the setting of his journey also illustrates the idea of isolation and how this can be detrimental to a person's reason and spirits.

c) The setting highlights the theme of isolation and injustice as Victor is imprisoned here away from his home country and falsely accused of the murder of Clerval.

PART FIVE: FORM, STRUCTURE AND LANGUAGE

Form [p. 65]

1 a) three; b) Walton; c) the monster to Victor; d) Victor to Walton

2 a) his sister Margaret; b) Walton; c) Victor, Walton; d) Elizabeth, Victor; e) Walton

3 The form of letters and first-person narratives from the main characters creates a sense of first-person testimony and therefore of authenticity. The letters bring a further sense of realism to the novel as they narrate key events from a different perspective to that of Victor.

Structure [pp. 66–7]

1 a) F; b) T; c) F; d) T; e) T; f) F; g) T

2 a) 2; b) 1; c) 5; d) 3; e) 6; f) 4; g) 7; h) 8

4

Point/detail	Evidence	Effect or explanation
1: *Victor's dream of Elizabeth foreshadows his wedding night.*	*'I embraced her, but as I imprinted the first kiss on her lips, they became livid with the hue of death'*	*This anticipates Elizabeth's death on her wedding night.*
2: *Elizabeth is linked to Victor's mother.*	*'I thought that I held the corpse of my dead mother in my arms'*	*Elizabeth changes into Victor's mother in the dream, linking Elizabeth's future death with Caroline's death in the past.*
3: *From the moment of its creation, Victor perceives the monster as a great threat to him.*	*'fearing each sound as if it were to announce the approach of the demoniacal corpse'*	*Victor's immediate response is to hide although there is no direct threat from the monster at this point. Victor's sense of danger foreshadows the threat the monster will later pose to Victor and his family.*

Language [pp. 68–70]

1 'evil spirit'; 'shrivelled complexion'; 'archfiend'; 'miserable deformity'; 'grave-worms crawling'

2 a) The verb suggests fear, and the adverb evokes the intensity of the emotion Victor feels.

b) The adjectives illustrate the considerable contradictions and contrasts that the monster begins to see in humans as he learns about them.

3 a) Victor is described as a noble ship that has been overwhelmed by a storm, indicating how he has been overcome by forces beyond his control.

b) This metaphor describes Victor's desire for knowledge as an unstoppable natural force, as strong and destructive as a powerful flood.

ANSWERS

5

Point/detail	Evidence	Effect or explanation
1: *The language emphasises how isolated Walton will be in a bleak and inhospitable landscape.*	*'I am going to unexplored regions, to "the land of mist and snow"'*	*This symbolises Walton's retreat from civilisation, something which Victor also pursues.*
2: *Nature imagery features heavily in the description of Victor's meeting with the monster.*	*'These sublime and magnificent scenes afforded me the greatest consolation'*	*The sublime setting inspires Victor, but also sets him apart from others and adds suspense and drama to his meeting with the monster.*
3: *The monster uses Gothic imagery to describe himself.*	*'archfiend'*	*The monster compares himself to Satan, conveying his sense of himself as evil and inhuman.*

PART SIX: PROGRESS BOOSTER

Expressing and explaining ideas [pp. 72–3]

2 Student A: High

Clear, relevant point with well-chosen quotations for evidence; specific words from the quotations are isolated and their effect explained. The student shows sound understanding of context in explaining the myth of Prometheus and relating it to the novel. The grammar and punctuation is to a good standard.

Student B: Mid

The explanation is reasonably accurate, but needs expansion. The student uses an expression that is presented as a quotation, but it is not from the text and this needs rephrasing. The writing is also rather clumsy.

3 The phrase 'the beauty of the dream vanished' suggests that Victor had originally great hopes for his creation, but they have now been completely dashed by the reality of what lies before him.

4, 5, 6

Shelley uses landscape in this chapter to **convey** how the monster and Victor are isolated from the rest of humanity. The text **demonstrates** that the scene is 'terrifically desolate' and the mountains 'admit of no escape'. This **reveals** how Victor and the monster are thrown together almost within a natural prison. Shelley **suggests** here how the two of them are locked together in a desolate struggle, and **indicates** how excluded they are from civilisation.

Making inferences and interpretations [p. 74]

1 Simple point: first sentence; develops: second sentence; inference: third sentence

2 b)

Writing about context [p. 75]

1 b)

2 c)

Structure and the linking of paragraphs [pp. 76–7]

1 Topic sentence: *Shelley presents Elizabeth as a saintly, beautiful and innocent young woman.*

Quotation words: *'sweet', 'celestial'*

Explains: *demonstrates her kindness and softness, indicates that she possesses an angelic quality*

2 Possible answer:

Shelley presents the monster in this chapter as motivated by a desire to seek revenge against humanity in general and against his creator in particular. His aim is to 'spread havoc and destruction'. The words 'havoc' and 'destruction' indicate the violence of the monster's intentions against all mankind, and as he gets closer to Victor he feels 'the spirit of revenge enkindled in my heart'. He is driven by an urge that he recognises as diabolical and he compares himself to Satan, stating that, 'I, like the archfiend bore a hell within me'. Through the term 'archfiend', the monster compares himself to Satan, while his reference to 'hell' within him suggests that the monster is far from revelling in the violence he contemplates, but rather that he is tortured by the painful and turbulent emotions he feels following his rejection by human society.

3 Topic sentence: *Shelley presents Walton as a highly determined, ambitious and somewhat idealistic character who resembles Victor in these respects.*

Change: *However, Walton also has fears about the demands of the trip.*

Links: *However, for example, and, in spite of*

Writing skills [pp. 78–9]

3 At the end of Volume One, Justine is put on trial for the murder of **William**. She is not able to explain how she came to have the **portrait** of Caroline and this is strong **evidence** against her. She is also forced into making a false **confession** and is eventually **executed** for the crime. The reader knows that Justine is **innocent** and that the monster in fact killed **William**.

4 Shelley's use of sublime imagery allows her to represent the power and desolation of the natural landscape. By placing Victor in this landscape, Shelley makes the reader more aware of his isolation. The landscape is described as terrifically desolate and its magnitude and grandeur are emphasised through the use of words such as 'immense' and 'magnificent'.

5 Student B

6 Shelley represents Old De Lacey as blind and this is important to two of the novel's key themes. Unlike the rest of the family, Old De Lacey is able to respond sympathetically to the monster. This allows Shelley to illustrate the themes of exclusion and prejudice.

Tackling exam tasks [pp. 80–1]

1 Explain how Shelley explores the theme of isolation:
- In this chapter
- In the novel as a whole.

Sample answers [pp. 82–5]

1 Student A: Expert viewpoint 1; Student B: Expert viewpoint 2

2 Student A: Expert viewpoint 2; Student B: Expert viewpoint 1